HOUSE OF WILKSHIRE BOOK 6

KATHI S. BARTON

This is a work of fiction. Names, characters, places, and incidents are products of the author's imagination or are used fictitiously and are not to be construed as real. Any resemblance to actual events, locations, organizations, or persons, living or dead, is entirely coincidental.

World Castle Publishing, LLC
Pensacola, Florida
Copyright © Kathi S. Barton 2020
Paperback ISBN: 9781953271402
eBook ISBN: 9781953271419
First Edition World Castle Publishing, LLC, November 23, 2020
http://www.worldcastlepublishing.com
Licensing Notes
Cover: Karen Fuller
Editor: Maxine Bringenbirg

Chapter 1

Cole had an idea of why he was sent on this trip. It was two women, and he was going to figure out which one was his mate. Or whether or not either one of them was. He wasn't making any predictions on this. If one of them were, then that would be all right with him. Either way, really, Cole didn't care.

Well, he did care, he supposed. Having a mate like the others would be a good thing. Not so much for him, but for whoever she was. The others would eat her alive if she was faint of heart. Laughing to himself as the plane landed on the tarmac, he wondered if any woman would be considered faint of heart. They all, as far as he could see, were bears when it came to fighting for something they believed in.

"Are you ready for this?" Noah had come along with him on this trip in the event they had any trouble. Cole was glad for the company but other than having witchy powers, he wasn't sure what sort of trouble he could get into that his dragon couldn't handle. "The faeries we brought with us are going to fix the back of the plane up for the one that is hurt."

"Ryan. Why do you suppose someone would call their daughter Ryan?" Noah told him what he knew. "So her name is Ryland. You do know that isn't that much better for a girl's name. Unless, of course, their father was named that."

"To be honest, I don't think anyone mentioned their names. Their parents, I mean. They're both gone, I guess. Killed in an automobile accident not long ago. I don't know what they do for a living, but Bryce told me that they were having trouble that the kids were left to deal with. I'm to look into why they didn't sue the drunk driver." Cole knew that, as well. Hopefully, he'd be able to figure it out while they were here. He didn't care for long plane rides when he could be flying as his dragon. "I just heard from Bryce. The brother is there with them. She said to bring him along too, but if we can help it, not to bring the wife. I guess she's a nightmare."

"Of course she is." They were told they could disembark now, and both of them got off the plane. "We're ahead of schedule. Would you like to get something to eat first? I'm starving. I missed dinner last night."

"Yes, I could eat. However, you're going to be the one to tell Kelly that we've not checked on her friends yet. When we boarded last night, she was telling me that they've had a really rough time of life. They not only lost their parents in an accident that took both their lives, but I guess some bills were left unpaid by them." Cole asked him if he thought they would win a suit against the driver. "I'd say that is a good possibility. I do know that the hospital bill for Ryan is being paid by the city."

Cole decided he'd grab something to eat at the airport. There were all kinds of places to eat, so he just got something from each of them that were open this time of the morning. He was munching down on the last breakfast sandwich when they pulled up in front of the hospital. Noah handed him a mint as they were let out of the limo.

"What are the chances, do you suppose, that this is going to go as easily as we hope?" Cole told Noah he didn't think it was going to go easily at all. "Yes, me either. There is just too much to go wrong. I mean, from what Bryce told me, Ryan's leg is not just broken but has some pretty deep bruising too. And some all over her body. The police that were at the bank just stood there and watched while he used a bat on her. Good thing he's dead. I think Kelly would have come here to end his breathing capabilities."

The hospital was busy, and Cole tried his best not to make eye contact with anyone. He didn't know why he did that when there were crowds of people around. He'd been doing it for so long now that he didn't even think about it much. Hearing someone screaming startled his dragon, but they made it to the elevator without anyone noticing them.

The floor the women were on was also busy, mostly with staff. Cole noticed that one of the rooms was being guarded, and he figured that was where they were. Instead of having to show them their identification, or anything for that matter, Noah told them they needed to take a break, and both of them left the door. That, Cole thought, was a very handy trick of magic.

Entering the room after a short knock, they found two people in the room with a doctor. The woman was sobbing. The man, easily related to the crying woman, was holding her hand. The doctor looked at them when he cleared his throat.

"I'm sorry. This is a private room." Noah told him to go on speaking. The doctor looked confused for a second but then turned back to the two people. "As I was saying, Rylie, there was more damage done to your sister's leg than we first thought. The bruising is going to take time to heal, but we're going to have to go in and put braces around her fibula bone to ensure that it's strong enough to even hold her weight. Then there is—"

"Stop." The three people in the room just froze. Noah looked at Cole. "I can heal the woman if she's not your mate. However, if they do it, there won't be any healing her. With the metal in her body, she'll have trouble for the rest of her life. Can you see if this sister is your mate?

That way, we can go and find Ryan and see what we can do to help her along."

"You mean I'm going to go down the hall or wherever and sniff out the women on this floor to see if anyone fits the bill to be my mate. That's ludicrous—you know that, don't you? There isn't any way that is going to work."

"Just sniff her so we can get on with what we came here for."

Cole walked over to the woman and leaned his head into her throat. He had a good mind to tell Noah he didn't smell anything, but he stood up. Then he sniffed the man.

"What is it? The guy? He's your mate?"

"No." He leaned into both their throats again. "This one is very sick. I'd say she knows it too. Cancer, if I don't miss my bet. The man here, I'm assuming he's the brother, is also in pain. However, it's not an illness with him, but he's been hurt badly. To be honest with you, Noah, that's all I can smell on either of them. Their pain."

"We need to find the sister. I don't know anything more than that we're supposed to bring them back with us. Kelly said to bring them all back healthy if we could. The only way to achieve that is to heal all three of them. Tell me what you know about Dillon." Cole moved his hand along his ribs and then the rest of his body. He looked at Noah. "Well? Is it bad?"

"Yes. Can I not tell you right now?" He asked him if he would heal. "Yes and no. I can heal him, but he's not going to be able to father children. Not after what was done to him."

"A doctor?" Cole only shook his head. "Christ. Don't do anything for him right now. Perhaps someone has an idea about what we can do for this guy. Wait. You go and find the sister. I'm assuming she's being prepped for surgery again. Try that. I'll take care of the sister here."

"All right." He started for the door, his heart breaking for this family. Even if he wasn't going to be mated into the family, he was going to do everything in his power to make sure they were healed, happy, and healthy. "I'm thinking that once she's healed, we can get out of here. Also, be on the look out for a woman named Sandra. Don't let her anywhere near any of them if she shows up."

Walking down the hall, he found that he was on the wrong floor for the surgery ward. Taking the stairs up, hating elevators more than ever today, he was on the right floor when he realized he hadn't thought about guards being up here. Telling Noah that he might be in trouble here, the two men there just simply walked away. He went into the room when he heard someone talking loudly.

"What the fuck do you mean, it's going to be a lot longer than you first told me about being under? Do you have any idea how that makes a person feel to wake up feeling like they've been on a fifty day drunk? Why can't you just, I don't know, numb it and do it that way?" The man standing by the gurney just sputtered about pain and manageability. "You took my gun away from me, or so help me, I'd show you what pain is like. Where is the fucking doctor?"

"Perhaps I can help you." Everyone in the room turned and looked at him. "I was sent here by her doctor to tell you that the surgery wasn't necessary."

"Who the fuck are you?" She could only be the sister to the two downstairs. Identical twins always gave him the willies. Cole didn't know why — they were just people — but this woman and the one downstairs were a perfect match. "Are you deaf? Who the hell sent you in here? They're supposed to be prepping me for the big cut up. They're going to slice open my leg from thigh to toes. Do you believe that shit?"

"I can make it so that is not necessary." He moved closer to the bed she was on. Looking around, he noticed that the two nurses were leaving, but the man, he thought he might be the anesthesiologist, was still standing there. "I was sent here by Kelly. My friend, Noah, he's downstairs with your sister and brother. Did you know they were both hurting?"

"What did you do to them?" He just stared at her. "Look, buddy. I don't fucking want to be here. I have shit going on that you'd not believe. My parents just died, I had to fucking kill a man yesterday, and now they're telling me I may not be able to walk without the assistance of a walker. That fucking sucks if you ask me."

"It does. But I'm afraid it's much worse than even they know. I can see your wounds, you see. They're going to cut you open, then they're going to see that not only is your fibula broken in two, but it's cracked in several places. Enough so that you'll need to have the bone replaced by metal rods. That I can't fix. I can fix broken, even shattered, but I can't put things back after they've been removed."

Ryan stared at him. She didn't ask him questions, like how did he know, or how could he see her wounds. Nor did she ask him how he could fix her. Instead, he watched her as she stared around the room and then at her leg. Cole didn't move closer. He waited for her to come to terms with whatever she was thinking.

"You said my sister and brother are in pain. Can you fix that as well?" He told her that Noah, his friend, was doing that now. "Dillon was telling us before I was brought here that he is getting a divorce. Is it Sandra that hurt him?"

"Yes. I can tell you how if you wish." She said, not just yet. "All right. Your sister is a little more tricky. She has cancer on the brain, as well as in her bloodstream. I don't believe she had much more than a few weeks, less than a month to live. I'm sorry about that. But as I said, Noah is fixing her."

"Thank you." She looked at him. "There are about fifty things going on in my mind at the moment. Nothing that I can say out loud without going into hysterics. And while you don't know me at all, I can assure you that it's not something I want to happen to me. I hate drama too."

"Good to know. I would very much like to heal you, Ryan. Also, before I get too close to you, I would also like to rule out whether or not you're my mate." She asked him what that would entail. "Just a smell of your neck. I might not be able to. I couldn't smell anything on your sister but her cancer. She smells of chemicals as well. If you are my mate or your sister is, there will be perks that all three of you will get. Immortality, for one thing. Never getting sick or hurt either."

"Are you setting me up for something scary? I don't scare easily. Rarely, as a matter of fact. I, for now at least, don't want to know what you are. I have a feeling you're not the run of the mill shifter." He told her he wasn't. "So, how does it work with you healing me? I'm assuming that either way, mate or not, you have plans to make it so that I won't have to walk with a cane for the rest of my life?"

"No. You won't. What it entails is that I give you a few drops of my blood. It won't hurt you — it will enhance you. However, I have no idea in what way. You see, there are six of us, all with mates except me. When they found their mates, things were shared with all of them." She asked if Kelly was enhanced. "She is. Very much so."

Ryan laid back and stared at him. He didn't squirm. There was a lot going on, and he was sure she had questions. But instead of voicing them, she told him something he'd bet few knew about her.

"I'm afraid. Not just of you. However, I am enough to wonder what I might be getting myself into, also of what will happen if I allow you to heal me. There will be a connection, even should we not be mates. Correct?" He nodded. "I thought so. I want to be able to walk, so please, do what you have to do to heal me. However, don't tell me yet if you're my mate or not. I'm sure you'll know, right?"

"Yes. As soon as I touch you." He didn't move forward. He was waiting for her to tell him it would be all right. While he was waiting, he heard from Noah.

We're all finished down here. Dillon is...the poor guy. Anyway, now that they're both up and about, they're packing up Ryan's things. Also, I need to make sure you know this — Sandra is in jail right now. I think we should be long gone before she's released. Is she your mate? He told him she was working up to allowing him to heal her. *Yes. Rylie said she never jumps in with both feet. I've told her nothing other than that she's healed. Also, I made sure she knows to talk to Ryan.*

I've told her they're both ill and that her sister has cancer. Noah thanked him. *I'm waiting for her to decide what she wants to do. I'm not rushing her. However, just so you know, I don't think I could even if I wanted. What about paperwork and such? Is that taken care of too?*

Since it was in the paper, I'm only saying that Ryan has been released. There won't be any way to trace her once she leaves with us. Cole told Ryan what he and Noah were talking about. *I'm calling for a ride to the airport. If you could at least get on with something there, we can be on our way.*

"If you could heal me, then I'm ready. As I said, don't tell me the mate thing just yet. I need to think." After taking the final steps toward her, Cole let his finger morph into a sharp claw and cut into his finger. "I'm thankful for you taking your time with me, but don't get used to it. I'm not easy."

"I never thought you would be."

As soon as Ryan opened her mouth, he let several drops touch her tongue. He could tell it was working as soon as she moaned. Stepping back from her, he watched it go through her system. In minutes, they were both on their way to the elevator that would take them to the lower floors and to the car. Cole didn't bother with sniffing her. He knew all he needed to know as soon as he helped her from the bed.

~*~

Rylie hadn't ever flown before. However, she had a feeling that flying in this plane was nothing like anything she'd ever fly in going commercial. The luxury in this sucker was nicer than any home she'd ever been in. Glancing at her brother, she wondered what he was thinking right now.

"You should know that I can feel your questions without you voicing them. Let it go, Rylie. I don't want to talk about it right now." She asked him if he'd ever be able to talk about it. "I don't know. I'm no longer hurting, and there isn't any reason for you to question me about it. Besides, having you know that I was hurt is bad enough."

"Can you at least tell me if Sandra is going to follow us?" He said not if he could help it. "Are you really going to divorce her?"

"I've already started the process." Dillon looked over at her. "I don't want to hear you say you told me so either."

"I'll fucking say it." They both looked at Ryan, who was sitting in the recliner with her leg up and resting. "I told you not to marry her. She's a fucking cunt. What was the straw that broke your back, Dillion? I think we should at least be privy to that much."

"If I tell you, will you fucking leave it alone?" Dillon rarely cursed. So when he did, it was funny to her. "I'm serious when I tell you that you're driving me crazy right now."

"I'll try to leave it alone, Dillon. But you should cut us some slack. If we didn't care, you'd be pissed about that as well." He said they never gave him a chance at that. "Fuck off. Tell us."

"This was just the start of things falling apart. Well, not the start, but what got me thinking I'm finished with her. When we got back home after the funeral, I was unpacking some of my things. I knew I was going to have to go back to help clear out our parents' home, so I left the things in there that I didn't need right away.

But I found so much more." Dillon bowed his head as if he were ashamed of something. "She'd been taking things from Mom and Dad's home and putting them in our luggage. The framed picture that you couldn't find of their wedding day? It was there too. Along with all the silverware that we couldn't find, and some of Mom's jewelry."

"Why, that fucking bitch. Did she tell you why she'd done it?" Dillon nodded at Ryan and told them. "What does that mean, she wasn't going to have you lose out? Lose out of what? Their bills? I don't want to sell any of the treasures, but divide it up between the three of us before we sell the rest. Her deciding to take those things made us all think that Mom and Dad had sold them off for cash. Now we know where they'd gone. What else did she take?"

"Two insurance policies that I have with me. There are some smaller items that I've also brought back. Some of their medications as well." Ryan asked him what he'd said to her. "I never got the chance. She...well, Sandra was pissed off about me saying I was bringing it back with me and attacked me. Then later, when I was asleep, she put me in the hospital. I've only just gotten out when Rylie called to say you were hurt. I took that opportunity to get away and hide out for a little while."

"Do you think she'll follow you to Kelly's home? I have to tell you, there won't be a better place to be safe than where we are headed." Rylie asked Cole why he thought that. With a glance at Ryan, he told her that it just was. "Not to mention, there are things you're going to find out when you get there that are going to be difficult to believe. Trust me when I tell you, we will not ever lie to you about things."

"That's a bold statement." Rylie knew that everyone lied. She didn't want either of these men telling them things that were simply untrue. "This trip, Kelly said she hoped that we'd stay. I'm assuming you all have money. Am I correct on that?"

"You are." If he was going to say anything more, his phone interrupted him, and he stood up to answer it. When he came back, he laid the phone on the table between them. "Kelly, you're on speakerphone now. Introduce the others to the people here."

"I'm Kelly, as you know. Here with me is Bryce, Nicole, Aisling, and... You know what, it doesn't matter. I'll just have them say who they are when they speak. I wanted to tell you a few things that you're not going to be happy about. Not that I care how unhappy you are with me; I love the three of you very much and want only the best for you." Ryan asked her what she'd done. "The bills your parents had are all paid off as of this morning. In addition to that, so is their funeral, as well as the cemetery plot they were buried in. Just so you know, that idiot at the funeral home is on my shit list. The house has the taxes caught up as well. My husband—he's a great guy, by the way—is looking into the accident to see why no one suggested that you sue the driver's insurance company. Unless, of course, you can tell me."

"I actually wondered that as well. We've been looking for an attorney that wouldn't take payment unless we won. It was pretty obvious that the driver ran the stop sign and hit them broadside." Kelly asked Ryan if she was aware that he was also stoned. "No. Drunk is all we were told. Our mom died on impact, and we were making funeral arrangements for her when Dad took a bad turn. We think it was because someone told him that Mom had died. Three days later, Dad passed away too. Not that his injuries weren't bad, but he might well have pulled through if he'd had it in his heart to do so."

"Devon, my husband, said he'll work with you on this." Ryan started to make a no doubt rude comment, but Rylie told her to hush. "I think you've just saved me a tongue lashing, Rylie. I so missed you guys."

"I've also some news on Sandra Cord. Christ, she's a nightmare." The woman speaking said that she was Bryce and was sorry. "I mean, you're going to divorce her, Dillon, so I'm assuming you know what sort of person she is."

"I do now. It's taken so many things going on to make me realize how right my sisters were in telling me not to marry her." Dillon laughed a little. "I'm assuming she's not all that thrilled about being in jail. The police officers that arrested her told me they'd never heard some of the words she'd strung together about me. What is it you found out?"

"Before I get to that, I want you to know that I've changed all the locks on your house and put someone there to keep an eye on it — also your home, Rylie. The only place I could find for you, Ryan, is an apartment you've not lived in for some time. I can have your place watched too if you want." Ryan told her she'd just sold her home before Mom and Dad had died. She'd been doing hotels since then. "All right. That explains a great deal. About Sandra. She's got herself an attorney. Her parents are paying for it. I don't know if you're aware of this or not, but they're as loony as she is."

"I thought they were both dead." Dillon looked at Ryan and her. "I had no idea that they were still alive. Sandra told me they had died when she was younger."

"They're both alive and kicking. Also, she has a brother that isn't anything like the others. A nice guy by all accounts. Stays away from the other three as much as he can. But back to Sandra. The attorney she has is going to find out that you're not one to fuck with, Dillon. At least since you became a part of this family." He asked why he was part of her family. "Once you were healed, as well as the others, you became a part of all of us. There will be more details when you arrive, but you're not going to have to worry about Sandra winning the suit she's bringing up toward you. She said that her little slice and dice of your nut sack is something that you did. Blaming her was just, and I'm quoting here, 'something that that dyke of a sister Ryan would have made you do.' Also, your wife thinks you're dumber than the dogs across the street. Which after looking into them, I can attest that they're nothing you want to be compared to in this."

No one said anything more about Dillon's wound, but Rylie had to wonder why Sandra would do such a thing to him. Rylie realized that another one of the women was talking. Paying attention to what was going on around her, she was sorry she'd missed it.

"I know that. Don't you think I'd be fucking aware that the president was looking for me? Christ, is there nothing you don't look into?" Ryan was all riled up again, and Rylie wondered who had done it this time. "He said that once I come back, he's going to talk me into taking the job. I am not now, nor have I ever considered being, in charge of a bunch of overpaid testosterone-filled assholes. Even the women, and there a lot of them, are on the take. I'm not going to mess with them. Fuck them. He made the mess. Let him fucking figure it out on his own."

"Oh, we're going to get along just fine, I think." Whoever was talking was laughing as she continued. "All right, people. Get some rest, and we'll talk when you arrive. Cole, if you'd pick up the phone now, I have a few things I need to tell you before you arrive."

When he picked up the phone and walked away, Rylie looked at her sister. She was glaring at no one in particular. Wondering what she was so upset about, she asked her to explain. Rylie didn't think she'd answer her, but when she finally did, she was just as shocked as she was to hear that the president's personal phone number was in Ryan's phone.

"One of us could be the mate to Cole." Rylie looked at the handsome man, then back at her sister. "I don't want to know right now. I have so much shit going on that having to deal with something more is going to make my head explode."

"What if I want to know?" Ryan nodded her head toward the man. "You ask him. Whatever happens, Ryan, at least we'll all be safe for a while. At least until we go back home. Is that what you're thinking? That you'll deal with it when you get home? You know as well as I do that it doesn't work like that. You know what we were told about shifters and mates."

"Don't you get it, Rylie? He's going to be into all of our lives. More than they are now." Rylie thought about that. Then she told her sister that so far, their being in their lives was working out pretty good. "Don't be an ass. Besides, I'm sure it's you. I mean, it would be great for you to have a nice handsome man that would be able to take care of you."

"You don't want the same for yourself?" She shook her head. "Why not? I mean, it might be nice to be pampered by someone for a change. Not that it matters, but they seem to have more money than sense."

She looked at Cole as he closed his phone. Having someone like him to wake up to daily would be nice, she thought. But the more she sat there thinking about it, all the things that she'd heard about mates, she decided it wasn't worth it. Having a man around would be nice some of the time. But someone around all the time? Well, she wasn't cut out for sharing her things any more than her sister was. No, it might be better off if neither of them knew who he might be mated to.

Chapter 2

Dillon loved being here. Not just because his wife wasn't—it was more than that. There was a quiet here that he could never obtain in the other place. There were no cars speeding by his home. Sirens blasting just close enough that you'd wonder if it was coming to your street. He'd bet anything that the crime rate here was zero.

When a shadow moved over his face, he looked up at who had disturbed his time. Smiling, he asked Matt to have a seat. The man was forever smiling. Dillon thought it had a great deal to do with the fact that he was married to a wonderful woman. That could make all the difference in the world.

"Are you going to be ready for tonight?" Dillon had forgotten about the big dinner. "We're a bit much when we're all in one house. I hope you're going to not be overwhelmed by it all."

"I'm sure I'll be all right. I've gotten around the others over the last few days. You're all a very close bunch, aren't you?" Matt told him they'd been friends for years. "I can tell. The women, they're close too. I noticed that they're trying to get my sisters involved in the things they're into. I don't know if you've noticed or not, but one of them is very stubborn. Also, I think Ryan can peel paint off a wall with her temper."

"I like them both. They're outspoken, which I find refreshing. Not to say that the others here aren't, but they're trying so hard to hold back that it makes me laugh." They both laughed at that. "I wanted to come and talk to you about a few things before we all get together. It's not all bad, so I can give it to you however you want it."

"I'd rather not hear it at all, but I know you've come all the way out here to tell me something." Dillon looked at the sea and felt his eyes fill with more tears. "I've been out here feeling sorry for myself for the last few hours. Not completely, but I know I've screwed up on life. My sisters, as I mentioned before, tried to tell me not to marry Sandra. Neither of them trusted her from the beginning. What has she done? I'm assuming some of the bad is because of her."

"It is." Dillon didn't rush Matt. He'd noticed that about all the men here—the women too. They weren't to be rushed into things when they had something to say. "The house you and her shared burned to the ground last night. There was no saving it. I'm so sorry."

"Before coming here, or at least before she tried to castrate me, I had moved all of my treasures out. Not that there were many of them. Things that I'd gotten from my family. Things I was given after my parents died. I didn't know, you see, that she'd do something like that. I only knew that if I left them at home, they'd be gone. Was anyone hurt?" Matt didn't answer him. "They're saying arson, aren't they?"

"Yes. It was ruled as arson. Two people were killed, I'm afraid. Not by the fire, but they were shot and then put into the house before it was set on fire. Your neighbors, Mr. and Mrs. Sandburg." Dillon let the tears fall. They'd been the nicest people he'd encountered since he'd left home. "I've spoken to the people in charge of the area, and they know you've been here since before it was started. The insurance company won't be able to pay out until they have someone arrested. They're looking for Sandra now."

"You said there was some good news too? I do hope that is the last of the bad." Matt told him there was only one more thing, but he was fixing that for him. "If you'd not mind, I'd like to just sit here a moment and absorb some of what you've told me. In the event that you're not aware of it, my life hasn't been a bed of roses. Being married to Sandra has been a nightmare from the very beginning. I guess you might say I've been ashamed for people to find out what it was like. She is abusive, both physically and mentally. I'm not sure how much you know about all of that."

"All of it." Dillon nodded. "I, as well as the rest of the family, would like to talk to you and your sisters about staying here with us. I have a job for you that I think you'll like. Rylie said you were an investment broker. I'd like to hire you…well, the family wants to hire you to take over the job of doing that for us."

"You have a great deal of money, I'm assuming." Matt only smiled. "I also think, and don't be upset with me if I'm wrong, but you're much older than you look. I don't know what you are, but you've been around for a good long time."

"Yes, we have. The men have." Dillon nodded. "We have a lot of money, Dillon. More than I think you've ever worked with. But what we need for you to take over for us is the money that is there for the charities we have. We'd like to be able to not have to keep putting money in if possible. We'd be able to do that, with your help, if you were to take the charity funds and reinvest them into more income for each of them. There are a great many of those as well, but we'd start you out slowly."

He thought about being here all the time. Dillon looked around, not just at the waterway this time, but all the other things that made him want to live here. The houses were modest. The yards large enough to have children playing in them. He could, if he wished, walk to town and have lunch, and any number of people would speak to him. It was what he thought of as a home town. Where you were known to everyone, and if you were smart, loved by them as well.

"I'll take it." Matt laughed and said he had thought he'd have to convince him. "I believe you might have some months ago. But I've had enough of rat races, getting to work on time, when all you want to do is rest. However, it's not only that. It's here. Being here the last few days has shown me that there isn't any reason to get all worked up about things that you have no control over. That's what I was doing with Sandra and my job. I was carrying around the stress of trying to keep my job, one I hated and making sure my wife didn't murder me."

"She would have." Dillon looked at the man. "Some of us can see bits and pieces into the future. You would have been dead by this time next week. It would have been a combination of an infection, as well as the strychnine she has been feeding you for the last year. It's out of your system as well, Dillon. When you were healed back at the hospital, that was taken from your body."

He cried. Dillon hated that he was so emotional right now. But these people had been nicer to him in the last several hours than his own wife had been their entire married life. Thinking about how she'd cut him, he decided to share it with this man. Even if he'd already found out what had happened, Dillon wanted to be able to voice it just this one time.

"I came home from work two weeks ago, exhausted

and ready to just fall into bed. But Sandra had been wanting to go out that night. It didn't matter that I don't dance, not even a slow dance. But she wanted it, and either I took her, or she'd just go on her own. That was the first time I'd ever just had enough. I told her to go then. After she left, I took a shower then went to bed." He thought about waking up in such pain. "I must have been more tired than I thought. Sandra had not only been able to gag me and tie my arms to the bed, but she'd also stripped me of my clothing. The stab to my inner thigh had me coming up from the bed and lashing out at her with my feet. I was only able to knock her back enough that I could move. Then she leaped on me—leaped on me like a fucking cat taking down prey. She managed to knife me in my scrotum twice before I was able to kick her in the head and knock her across the room."

"The police said you were able to get the gag off. Had she been only a quarter of an inch more to the right, you would have bled out." Dillon said he'd been screaming around it for a while, and it finally moved off his mouth. The doctors had told him several times how lucky he'd been. "I'll say. I don't know how you were able to get up to call for an ambulance. The police, they've arrested her for attempted murder. Our women are working on other crimes they believe she was a part of to make the case against her stick. Ryan is also calling in favors to have her not get bail."

"What are you?" He looked away and then back.

"I know you're not human, as I said before. I'm really curious as to what sort of person you are. And are you all the same?"

"I'm a dragon." Dillon thought he was joking and asked him if he was. "No. I'm a dragon, as are the other men you've met. Devon, he and Kelly are the king and queen of all of us."

"Seriously?" Matt laughed and nodded. "I have to be honest with you. I thought you were something I'd have a hard time believing. However, I never in my life thought of a dragon. I bet it's wonderful to soar through the sky without a care in the world. Are you…? I'm not sure how to ask this, but how large are you? I'm assuming you're about the size of a small SUV."

"Much larger. A great deal larger. Devon is bigger than any of us, as you can well imagine, being the king and all." Matt turned to the castle behind him. "If I were to shift and stand next to the castle, I'd be a little taller. About twenty feet taller."

"Christ." They both laughed. "You said that Devon is larger? My goodness, it must be a sight to see you six in the sky."

"Kelly is a dragon as well. Would you like a rundown of what the women are? It's pretty awesome that we have all this power." Dillon told him to tell him. "Kelly, as I said, is a dragon. Bryce is a witch. Not just a witch, but the grand witch of all. Her familiar is, of course, her husband, Noah. Not too many people mess with her in the first place, but with Noah there, she's never been bothered. Nicole is a wonderful cook, as well as the protector of all of us. She and Jackson will also assist Devon when he has to deal with one of the others. Let me think. Connor and Roxanna are necromancers. To be honest with you, I thought them all gone. People would kill them not for what they could do but for the trouble they could cause if they were to bring up someone they knew. But they do an amazing job, even just helping the dead with some issues they might well have."

"You and your wife, what is it you do?" Matt laughed. He told him what they were. "A dragon of the elements? I don't think...well, I can figure it out. I'm assuming you can control them. All the elementals."

"That's it precisely." Matt put out his hand, and a stream of water rose up from the earth to his palm. While he spoke, he played with the water as if it were nothing more than a long rope. "I'm a very rare type of dragon. My body, if taken apart, is worth more than even Devon's, with all his power. Aisling is a white dragon. What that means for us is that as soon as we bonded, she became exactly what I am. Our children will also be a pure as we are since we were both born dragons."

"You said taken apart. I'm assuming you mean that people would kill you to harvest your body." He felt his face heat. "I didn't mean that to sounds so heartless. I just meant—"

"I knew what you meant. And yes. That is the sole

reason there aren't more of us around. We helped the human population a great deal when they needed us. Then at some point, it was discovered that there was magic, a great deal of it, to be had if we were cut up. Witches and warlocks are especially hard on us." Dillon told him he was sorry. "No need to be, Dillon. None at all. There is something else that I need to make you aware of if you've not already been told. We all believe that one of your sisters is Cole's mate. He won't say if they are or not. Cole made a promise to Ryan that he'd not tell her until she wanted to know. And by doing that, he's not told any of us anything."

"Is it important that we all know?" Matt told him it was because they'd have to protect her better. "Better than you are now? You do know that I've never seen a family more prepared for anything that comes their way than you guys. But I have to warn you. All of you. Whichever sister it is, it's not going to be an easy coming together. Both of them have been hurt badly by men."

When Matt didn't say anything, he didn't either. They'd find out soon enough. Dillon knew too that it wasn't his story to tell. It would have to come from his sisters. He did wonder if anyone had looked into their minds. He, in some little way, would love to be able to see what had actually transpired when they'd been hurt. But then, Dillon wasn't sure he wanted to know. It would break his heart all over again to hear more than they'd shared with him. While he knew it had been brutal, he also knew they were much stronger than even he gave them credit for.

~*~

Ryan tossed her cell phone in the trash can by the store she was just about to enter. Pulling it out, she took out the sim card then busted the sucker into three pieces. One of the things she had gotten from Cole when he'd helped her along was a good deal more strength. It had come in handy over the last few days.

"You must be Rylie." Ryan told the woman that she was Ryan. "Ah, the very one I was looking for. My name is Susanna. I'm the grandmother to Devon. I've been away for a few weeks and have only just heard that we have visitors. How are you enjoying our little town, my child?"

"It's lovely. Quaint, I guess someone might call it." Susanna smiled at her and told her to tell her what she really thought of the town. "I'm not sure, actually. This is the first time I've been able to leave the house without fifty armed people with me. I'm a loner, and all this protection shit is driving me over the fucking edge."

"Have you had lunch?" Ryan told her that was next on her list. "Will you need to retrieve that device? I'm sure that since you tossed it away, you don't wish to speak to the person on the other end."

"No, I do not. Not any of them." She followed the woman to the deli she'd been wanting to try since they were brought here. "I'm not sure what is going on, but everyone is acting all weirded out that my family is here. Not weirded out, I guess, but super friendly. Why?"

"Well, I'd like to say that they're normally that friendly, but I don't think you'd believe me. However, they are. And since you've become a part of the household, I'm sure they're trying their best to make a good impression on you." Ryan asked her if it was because she might be in the running to be a slave to Cole. "Slave? I doubt very much he'd treat you so if you were his mate. Cole is a good young man. He's had a little bit of trouble that has been resolved, and I do believe he's doing better for it."

"My brother, Dillon, is going to stay here. I don't know what Rylie and I are going to do. I guess we'll figure that out when I'm brave enough to ask if it's me or Rylie that is the mate to Cole. There is just too much going on in my head for me to even think that any of this is real. I mean, this is the most laid back town I've ever been to. Usually, when a town is this way, I immediately think they're harboring a serial killer or something. But I don't get that vibe here." Susanna laughed, and it made her smile. "I'm not one for society, really. I didn't date much in high school. I didn't even go to my own graduation. Rylie did. She's the outgoing one of the two of us."

"Would it be so bad if you were his mate, Ryan?" Ryan looked away, pretending to look at the specials written on the chalkboard. "I'm going to take that as an undecided. I've known Cole all of his life. He was forever here after Devon's father was killed. I believe all of them have stayed with him in that castle more than they did at their own homes. They've all had very tragic and horrific childhoods. The women, too, have had some rough times in their lives."

"I've heard some of them. Kelly talks about how she fell in love with you long before she met Devon—who I like, by the way. He's sort of stodgy when he wants to be but can laugh at himself too. I like that. All of them have some kind of quirkiness that I think is funny. It suits them. They're old world, aren't they?" Susanna asked her if she knew what they were, the people she was living with. "No. I asked Cole not to tell me anything. I don't know that I could handle much more. Or at least I hadn't been able to before. But now that I'd like to know, I don't know how to get him to answer me. Even if I knew how to ask him. I've been avoiding him."

"He told me. That's one of the reasons I've come to town to find you. To see if you're doing all right or if you need anything. He's also said that if you wish to know what he is, I may tell you. As for whether you're his mate or not, that will have to come from him. Would it be so bad being a mate to him? Or for your sister to be?" Ryan had been muddling that same question in her head since they arrived. "What is it that I can answer for you, Ryan? I'm open to many subjects that you could want to talk about."

"I'm afraid." She looked at the other woman, wondering if she'd have any better luck telling her what she was afraid of than she had her sister. "I have absolutely no trust for people in general. Rylie and Dillon, of course, but not even my parents. They weren't terrible people, but they weren't the kind of parents you'd go to if you had a bad day or if you were hurt. I'm not saying they didn't love us. I'm sure they did. But I think that had we not been born, they would have been much happier. After they died, Rylie and I found some information that they'd, at one time, decided to give her and I up for adoption."

"But they didn't." Ryan told her why they'd not been able to. "So, because no one could guarantee that the two of you would stay together, they decided to not go through with it. I can understand that, I guess. At least they wanted the two of you to grow up as sisters."

"I suppose. I've actually thought of that too. Then after Dillon was born, they tried again. We were four years old when he was born. I don't know why they thought they'd have any better luck keeping the three of us together in an adoption any more than they did when it was just Rylie and I, but that was there on the signed paperwork as well." She looked at the other woman. "What are all of you?"

"Dragon." Ryan had known it was going to be something special. Something that no one believed in anymore. While dragon hadn't been one of the things she had thought of, it didn't really surprise her. "You don't seem all that surprised. Did someone else give you a hint?"

"No. I mean, not directly. I was in the hall of paintings this morning. There are some of the best paintings I've ever seen, by the way. There is a dragon in each of the paintings. Not right out in the open, but something you'd have to look for." Susanna seemed surprised she'd seen them. "I didn't touch any of them. I just got turned around and ended up there. Benshaw found me there and even gave me a tour of the others that have been moved for restoration."

"The simple fact that you saw the dragons in the paintings is what surprised me." Ryan asked her what that meant. "I think you know the answer to that without me having to explain it. Not everyone can see them. No one but immediate family."

When her meal was set in front of her, she just stared at it before she looked at Susanna. She was enjoying her meatball sub and talking to one of the waitstaff. After Susanna introduced her to the young woman, the server went on her way and left the two of them there. Ryan didn't know how to ask the next question.

"Of course you do, dear. You can even speak to Cole if you wish. Just think of him and then speak, as you would thoughts. I do believe he's working on the house he only recently was given. An incentive the women purchased for him so he'd stick around." Ryan wasn't sure she wanted to speak to him right now. Susanna told her that was all right too. "I'm sure that what you've only just figured out will wait. I've not told him, but just so you know, he can feel your uncertainty. He's asking me if you're all right with him being a dragon."

"Why would that matter?" Susanna shrugged as Ryan picked up her sub too. "Men are such pussies at times. Why would he ask you if I was all right when I'm sure that, as you said, he could speak to me. Dumbass."

I didn't want to startle you when I just spoke to you. She nearly did scream when it sounded like he was right there behind her. *Susanna said you've seen the dragons in the portraits in the great hall. I believe there are more of them. I have quite a few of them myself of my —*

Shut up a second. I'm thinking. His laughter made her feel warm and fuzzy. *Don't you have something better to do with your time than to annoy me? I mean, I'm having a nice lunch with Susanna.* She thought about the ramifications of being his mate. *I'm not sure what I should do now.*

What would you like to do? She asked him straight up if she was his mate. *You are. I think you've known it for a little while now. You can do things with the magic I shared with you that your brother and sister can't do. I'm assuming you've been thinking of ways to get out of being my mate as well.*

You'd be better off with my sister than with me. She's more your style. Cole asked her what she thought her style was. *Mine? Well, I'm not nearly as nice as Rylie is about things. I tend to just do whatever needs to be done, and Rylie overthinks it. I think that's the tradeoff we got being identical twins. Will you be able to tell us apart? Most men can't.*

I can tell who you are, even with you standing next to your sister. Not just the way she talks, though that is a hoot to me. But also the way you stand. Did you know that you give off the appearance of being relaxed all the time? Rylie sits all prim and proper. You sit like you want. If you're sitting to rest, you slouch down in the chair and sigh heavily. If you're unsure of yourself, you sit stiffly and have your right hand free. I'm assuming so that you can reach for your gun if you need it. There are other things I can tell you about yourself, but I'd like to be in person when I do that. She told him not to be nice to her. *I'm a nice man, Ryan. And believe it or not, I've fallen in love with you. I know it's too soon for you, but I wanted you to know that.*

I've been hurt before. I'm terrified of sex. He asked her if she'd been raped. *Shouldn't you know that? I mean, everyone and their butler around here has been inside of my head like I'm a bag of candy on Halloween. Christ, I'm overwhelmed again.*

Just breathe love. In and out. She growled at him. *I'll have to show you how I growl. It's very scary. However, you should know that I'd never harm you. Never take advantage of your nature. Also, I won't look into your head unless you don't answer me. I know you've been hurt. It's in every move you make. But I'm a patient man, and I can wait until you're ready for me to know. I'm here for you.*

I don't know that I'll ever be ready for anything. Ryan asked him not to say anything. *I need to think. Just think about things this will change for me. I'm guessing everything, but I have to think.*

All right. You take all the time you need. However, you should know that now you've acknowledged us, I'm going to be hanging around you more. Not only do I want to be close to you, but my dragon does also. She asked him what the dragon would want of her. *Nothing more than you're willing to give him. Neither of us wants anything from you other than your love. And we can wait on that as well.*

Ryan didn't know how to tell him she wasn't any more sure of love than she was of anything else in her life. She would need to speak to him. To tell him what she had on her mind. Also, about what the fucking president wanted from her.

When lunch was over, the two of them went in and out of the shops. They were gearing up for the warmer weather now. There were seeds in the stores on big displays, as well as tools. Ryan asked why they weren't in seed packets like they had back home.

"These seeds are handed down from family to family. They only sell them when they have too many. But you'll also see that everyone is generous with the food they grow. We are as well with the castle foods. Most everyone here is self-sufficient in some way or another." Ryan told her how she'd been in the new courthouse just yesterday. "Yes. The entire town was in on building it. There are renovations going on all over our little town. If you'd like, I'm sure the others would gladly have you get in on some of the projects."

"I'm not too crafty or anything like that. I'm more of

a 'you tell me what to do, and I'll do it' sort of helper."
They both laughed. "Again, Rylie would be good at
something like that. She used to do flower arrangements
when she was younger. Also, Dillon. He's very handy
with manly projects. He built me a shelf that was a huge
selling point when I sold my house. I really hated to leave
it behind, but I had nowhere to take it. Not to mention, it
was fucking huge."

The two of them ended up back at the house. Susanna
had pointed out the street that the house Ryan and Cole
owned was located on. She wasn't so sure about that.
The homes were bigger than her apartment building, and
then some. She didn't want to see it, not with Susanna.
Ryan wasn't even sure she wanted to see it with Cole. But
for the first time since they arrived here, she was looking
forward to perhaps living here permanently. Ryan hoped
she could convince her sister to live here as well.

Chapter 3

Ryan wasn't thrilled about her brother having to go back and testify against Sandra. It scared her that he might well get hurt. Sandra, as she'd been saying for some time, was unstable. She nearly got up to go back outdoors, a place she was enjoying a great deal, when all the women, all six of them, came into the room and sat down with her.

"Something has happened." Kelly nodded, then looked around the room at the others. "Tell me. Don't beat the bush to death in getting there, either. I'm not in the mood, nor do I want to have to figure out where this is going. I think it's really sweet of you guys to come here and be here for me. But I'm not going to be happy if I have to beat the shit out of you to get the answers."

Roxanna smiled before speaking. "We're waiting on your brother and sister, as well as Cole. He needs to be here since this essentially affects him as well."

Ryan thought of all the things they could say to her. Whatever it was, she knew she wasn't going to be able to ignore it. As soon as Dillon and Rylie arrived with Cole, she moved to sit with him and held his hand when he offered it. It wasn't until the rest of the men showed up that she felt calmed. She wondered if they could hold her too.

"We've been notified by a couple of people. I want you to know that I didn't call them. They called me to—" Connor cleared his throat. "I've spoken to your parents. They wanted me to tell you what they know about their deaths."

"Sandra killed them, didn't she." It wasn't a question, but Roxanna said she had, but there was more. Ryan wasn't sure that she wanted to hear more but continued. "All right. I don't even know why that was the first thing I thought of. What did she do? Do you know?"

"I'm going to start at the beginning of what I know. That way, I can fill you in on what we've all been able to figure out. Is that all right?" Ryan looked at her sister when she said yes. Dillon looked like he'd been hit between the eyes with a bat. "All right. Just before you married Sandra, she took out a million dollar policy on your parents. I can't figure out why she did that way back then, but it has kept the insurance people from jumping to conclusions. The policy is doubled since they were killed in an accident. To be honest with you all, I had no idea that she was that smart."

"She's collected two million dollars? On the death of our parents? Did you know she tried to steal some of the things that belonged to them before they were even cold in their graves? Please tell me you have a plan." Bryce told her not as yet. Also that she'd not collected it because she'd been in jail since she'd been home. "So she will get it. All that money. You said she killed them. Is there a way we can prove this?"

"Not as yet. But we'll get to that." Ryan told Bryce she was sorry. "Don't be, Ryan. We're all working on this, and I promise you that things will come out ahead for you guys in the end. The man in the car that was supposed to have driven into your parents told Roxanna he'd been murdered by Sandra as well. That he'd been just sitting in an alley waiting— Never mind. That doesn't matter. She killed him, put him in the car, and then took him to the intersection to wait for your parents to go by. They were predictable, you see. Every Friday night, your parents would go to the same restaurant, and she knew the time they'd be coming by. Ramming into them was easy, I guess, as she only had to make sure the gas pedal was pushed hard enough to slam into them."

"That didn't kill them, did it?" Dillon shook his head when Roxanna said that it hadn't. "She murdered them when they didn't die in the accident. Probably because they might take too long to die for her to collect. Christ, I wish every day that I'd just listened to everyone and not married that bitch."

When Dillon started to stand, it was Devon that went to him. Ryan didn't know what he said to her brother, but he did sit down with them once again. She asked Bryce what it was that they could do.

"This is what we've come up with. It's a solid plan, and it will work. I'm of the opinion that Sandra is not nearly as smart as she thinks she might be. Also, this I've heard from several people; she also has a high opinion of herself. Is that about right?" They all three agreed. "Good. When we get to the courthouse, and we'll all be there with you, I want you to not press charges against her."

"Let her go, you mean." It was Cole who answered, telling Dillon that wasn't it. "Then, I don't understand. Do we want her to collect the money before we step in? Tell me what you have planned, and I promise you, I'll do whatever it takes."

"You're going to love this one."

After Cole explained what he wanted Dillon to do, Ryan could see that it might well work. Not only did Sandra hate to be proven wrong about anything she said, but she also had a hot temper when someone interrupted her when she was speaking. It would be fine if she did that to whoever she was talking to. But she lost it when you'd cut her off in favor of your own opinion. It didn't even matter to her if she was wrong. Just don't interrupt her.

They were leaving tonight to go to the courthouse. Ryan had thought it would only be the three of them, but she was so much happier to know they'd be all there in force. Not only would it show that they were all behind what Dillon was supposed to do, but also that they were going to be there for him forever.

Ryan packed an overnight bag and sat on the edge of the bed. She'd been staying with Kelly and her husband since she'd arrived. She looked at the doorway when someone cleared their throat, she smiled at Cole.

"Are you ready to go? I know they said we'd only be there for a short time. But I was wondering if you wanted to take care of the things you left at the hotel and at your sister's." She patted the side of the bed. "Are you going to tell me you'd rather I didn't go?"

"No. Christ, no. I was going to ask you some things I've been thinking about. If you'd rather stay there, that's fine too." He nodded and moved into the room. However, instead of sitting on the bed, he sat on the floor in front of her, stretching out his legs in front of him. She smiled at him again. "You're very comfortable with your body, aren't you?"

"Yes. I mean, it's been mine since I can remember." She laughed when he did. "Ask away. I'm here for you in whatever you want to know."

"Your home. It's huge, isn't it?" He told her how large it was. "Christ. Do you plan on filling that with children? I know the two of us might not be able to have kids of our own. Your sisters-in-law have been giving me tidbits of information every time I see them. It's been both helpful and annoying, as you can well imagine."

"I can. They're pushy. No, we might not be able to have our own children, but I don't care about that. I'd be happy just to be able to raise them with you. Ask me what you're trying to avoid." She asked him the first question. "Do I want you to work? That's not my decision. I have a feeling you enjoy working for the sake of staying busy. Same as myself. I can't stand to be idle. Does that answer your question?"

"It does. So, do you think we can see your home before we leave?" He corrected her. "Okay, if you say so—our home before we leave? I'm very nervous about what you might expect me to do as the head of a household. That's what Kelly told me I'd be doing. Running a very large home with an endless supply of money to make it work. That scares me a little."

"It shouldn't. Yes, while not endless, we do have income that is more than most people make in a years' time coming in daily. And you'll have a staff that will answer only to you. I know you're neat and like things in order." He snapped his fingers. "I have someone that would like to work with you. Every dragon has a faerie they use for all kinds of things. I have one as well. Right now, she's getting the staff ready for you to meet them. Your faerie, should you want him, is Watson. I believe he got his name from a television show. I think at one time he was going by Brown. This, I believe, suits him much better."

Cole asked her to put out her hand. When she did, the tiniest little person she'd ever seen flew to her and landed there. Pulling him closer to her face to get a good look at him, he bowed low and told her his name.

"My lady. I must say you are a very beautiful creature." She thanked him. "I can do things for you that you might need me to do. I will also protect you with my life. And before you think to yourself what is a little person going to do to protect me, then I shall show you."

All he did was whistle. It wasn't a tune or any kind of music other than a shrill sound. Before she could ask him what that was supposed to do, Ryan noticed they were no longer alone in the room. It was, quite literally, filled with more of the tiny people. But they were armed with swords and at the ready. It was the only way she thought to describe what they looked like to her.

"That was really fast." Watson told her they were forever ready. "I can see that. But what if I'm kidnapped or something like that? How long will it take you to assemble? Also, if it is all right with you guys, I'd like for some of you to be watching out for my sister and brother. They're all the family I have left, you know."

"We're your family too, mistress." She felt her face heat up when Watson pointed that out to her. "Also, Lord Cole here. He's a big dragon, you know, and will protect you better than even we can."

"I'm sorry." Cole told her it was fine. He was something to get used to. "I'm sorry. I didn't mean that either. I'm just not used to people being...I'm not at all used to people being nice to me. I'm sure I can get used to it. You've been the nicest man I've ever met, to be honest with you. I'm sort of waiting for the other shoe to drop, you might say. It's like I've been waiting my entire life for it to drop, and it usually does."

"Thank you." Cole stood up and pulled her from the bed. "Come on. We'll go and see the house and see what sort of changes you'd like to make to it."

When they went into the back yard, she wondered if they were going to walk. But when he stepped back from her, several feet, she had to wonder what he was up to. Watson landed on her shoulder and told her not to scream. It was all the warning she got before she was staring at a huge dragon.

Unsure what she was supposed to do with him levitating about ten feet from the ground, she asked the dragon if he could hear her. Sitting down on the lawn, she watched as the big creature not only sat down but laid down on the grass so that his nose was right in front of her. Their size difference was just too much to ignore. Ryan refused to be afraid of his dragon and put out her hand to touch him. She was amazed at how hot his breath was.

"I was just thinking about how hot you are, and I would imagine that your breath would need to be hot.

Can you blow fire over things?" He told her he could. "I wondered how I was going to know what you were saying. So you can connect with me as well."

I can. We are different, my human and I. You can talk to either of us if you wish. Or both. 'Tis up to you. She nodded. Putting her hand to his nose, she could feel that he was hard, like a rock. He was also covered in ridges all over where she could see him. *I am covered in scales so that nothing can pierce my heart. And when it is necessary to protect all that I love, I can change yet again and be covered in my armor. One that is dangerous for you to be this close to. I shall show it to you the next time.*

"I'd like that." She moved to where his legs were under him. One of his claws, bigger than she was as it lay flat on the ground, seemed to be dug deep into the earth so that she couldn't see the tip. "I would imagine you can claw your way out of almost anything with these. They're very sharp, aren't they?"

The dragon pulled the paw, she thought was what it might be called, from the dirt, and she could see that it went well deeper into the earth than she'd thought. Touching her fingers to it, she was careful of the small blades on the nail. Ryan wondered at the few that were missing. He must have been injured when he was helping the humans when he was younger.

"What shall I call you?" He asked her what she meant. "You said you're separate from Cole the man. Do you have a name I can call you if I need you? I don't know what that would be when I would need you, but it would be nice that I can call you to protect us both should something happen to Cole."

You may call me Dragon if you wish. Or any name you can think of. But if you were to call for me, calling for your dragon, I would think it would be much scarier to the people that will be dead soon after I come to you. She smiled at him as she walked around to the other side of his large head. *Do you trust me, mistress?*

"I'm not sure. I don't not trust you. Does that make sense?" He said he didn't understand. "I trust that you won't crush me. I also trust that you will not eat me. But other than that, I don't know what I feel toward you. Will you be loyal to me?"

Forever. She hadn't expected that answer from him and stepped back from him so she could see into his eyes. They, too, were bigger than her entire body. She asked him if he'd protect Cole over her. *No. Without you, there will be no Cole. Without you around, there will be no reason for us to draw our next breath. If something should happen to you, be it harmed or worse, I shall only wish to lie down to never rise again. I will have failed you in keeping you safe, and I will not be able to live with myself should I let that happen.*

She popped him hard on the nose. "That's the stupidest thing you could have ever said. What if I fall down the stairs? Or turn my ankle because I wasn't paying attention? What would you do then? Still lay yourself down and die?" She smacked him a second time and saw tears fill his eyes. "Did that hurt? I hope so. Because when you say things like that, you hurt me as well. You cannot think I'll be all right with you laying down your life for me because I'm clumsy."

Perhaps I was wrong about protecting you, my lady. Perhaps it should be you that is protecting us. His laughter echoed into her head. *You are a hero to me. A warrior that will protect all that you love. Yes, I will be there for you and will not lie down and die because you might have slipped.* He stood up over her. His body was as large as any building she'd ever been around. *I shall show you the world.*

Before she could know his intentions, she was being picked up by the dragon. Holding on tightly to the very claws that had scared her just a little, she felt the wind from his wings surround her. The trees swayed back and forth from the tremendous amount of force he was making. When they were high in the sky, she could see so much from the perch in his hand.

~*~

Cole would have flown around the world if they'd had the time. Her laughter coming from his palm had made him feel like he'd never felt before. When they'd landed in the yard not long ago, the one behind their home, he could feel her disappointment as if he were wearing it. He was going to make sure he took her on all kinds of short rides so she'd be as happy as she'd made him.

"The kitchen is huge, isn't it? I can cook, but I don't

enjoy it. I guess the others know how to cook. The other dragons, I mean." He told her they all learned to cook from Devon's grandma. "Susanna is a wonderful person. But you can't let that stodgy appearance fool you. She can be mean when she needs to be. Oh, look at this, Cole. It's a wonderful window."

"It wasn't here when I moved in. Some of the faeries asked if they could make some changes to the place, and since I'd not met you, I told them to have fun. This is the lady of the earth, if I remember. I've not seen her in a very long time." The mural was simply breathtaking. It was so colorful he almost didn't want to stop looking at it. Cole did look at Ryan. "They'll change it out if you don't care for it."

"You'd do that, wouldn't you?" He nodded. "No. I love it. But I can tell you right now, this isn't going to work if you don't tell me your feelings too. You can't be thinking I'll just go along with you not having opinions about shit. If you like this, then say, 'I really like this and would like for it to stay.' Believe it or not, I'm not a monster."

"I know you're not. My plan is to make this place so nice you'll want to live here with me forever." She said nothing as she moved out of the kitchen toward the dining room. Cole looked over at Faith when she tisked at him. "What? I'm trying to make sure she's happy."

"Yet you pissed her off. Do you not have opinions other than the ones that she has?" He said he did. "Then you should tell her them instead of thinking to revolve the world around her. I don't think she'll care for that any more than any of the other women in this family would."

"I think you might be right." Faith tisked at him again. "Now what I have I done wrong? I'm going to work on this. I swear it."

"I've no doubt that you will, my lordship. Yet your mate is in the other room crying." He asked why. "I'm sure it has something to do with you being such a...I believe it is called a wishy-washy person. She needs strength more than she needs you to be such a...pussy about things. I am learning new words from Lady Bryce and the other women."

"Yes, well, you should look those words up before you use them." She said she had, and she thought they suited him just fine. "I've never had a mate before. I'm sort of learning as I go in this."

"You should learn faster before she takes a bat to your head. My lord." He had a feeling he was going to have to tell Faith not to hang out with the others for a while. She was beginning to sound like them more and more. "Also, she has something to tell you. It will break her heart to have to tell you as well. Do not look for it. It is her story to tell. Not one for you to look into and jump to conclusions. In this, I believe that you shall."

"Is that what makes her scream at night? The thing she must tell me?" She nodded and looked toward the doorway where Ryan had gone. "I'm in love with her,

Faith. There is nothing I'd not do for her. Ever."

"Sometimes it's not what you do for someone that they need you for, your lordship. But that you are willing to listen to the story until it is finished. I think you to be safer should you try that once in a while." Cole asked if he should ask her about it. "Nay. You do that, and she will not trust that you've not looked on your own. Just allow her to come to you. She will when she trusts you as much as I do."

"You think that will be soon?" Faith said that would be up to her. "Yes, all right. I'll wait. But I don't like it."

"Of course you do not. As I said before, you are a most impatient man when it comes to getting things done. It is what brought you down once before. Remember that?" He told her he did, then shivered at the memories of it. "I remember it as well. You will need to be calm before you break your heart, and in turn, break hers as well. Calm. Say it with me. I will stay calm from now on."

He repeated it several times as he made his way into the dining room. Ryan was sitting at the long table there and talking to a few of the faeries. When they saw him, they smiled larger than he'd ever seen them smile before. Cole sat down at the table across from her and waited for her to tell him what was going on.

"I've fallen in love with this room, but I don't think it's wide enough. I mean, it has this beautiful table here that Watson was telling me you've had for a long time. But there is very little room on either side of it to walk around. See?" She got up and pulled the chair out again to about the width of someone sitting in it. She was right, there was barely enough room for her to get behind the chair, and she was tinier than he was. "I would think if there were enough people in here, the other dragons especially, there would be no room for anyone to be served. They're going to see about expanding this room. I don't know what that would entail, but they said it would be a piece of cake."

"Have a seat over here and watch."

She moved toward him without any hesitation. As soon as she was seated, the faeries, about a thousand of them, moved to the wall Ryan wanted to be enlarged, and the wall disappeared. After that, they managed to put in bigger windows with murals in them, including the top, as they moved the wall out several feet. The entire room looked like it was built this way rather than just being remodeled. Even the table he'd always thought too narrow was widened and fit nicely with the bigger room.

"There you go. And I love the addition of the windows too. They alone make the room look much larger."

Ryan got up and moved to the windows. She and Watson, who seemed to be in charge of the addition, talked for a few moments before he moved toward the other faeries. In seconds, the windows were floor to ceiling, and there were now two large corner cabinets that Cole just realized were going to be needed.

"This looks amazing. I have some china that I think

would look great in those new cabinets." She turned back to him and smiled. "I could live with you smiling at me like that for a very long time. What do you say about you moving in here? There are plenty of bedrooms if you don't want to sleep with me until we get to know one another better. That way, you can get a feel for the house and what you want to be done to it."

She stood there for several minutes. He waited. Whatever she was thinking about, it took away her smile and made the area between her pretty brows wrinkle. It was all he could do to stay seated and not want to hold her. When she sat down across from him, he finally asked her what was hurting her.

"Will you just listen to what I have to say?" He nodded, then explained how it would be difficult for him to keep that a promise. "I understand that. All the men are like that in this family. They're the dragons that want to slay anything or anyone for the people they love. And you do love me, don't you, Cole?"

"I do." She put her hands on the table and took his into hers. "I'm here for you, darling. I promise whatever it is, the two of us can talk about it, and you can tell me who I have to slay for you."

That made her laugh. Then the sadness was back. "Rylie and I never went anywhere without the other. It wasn't, I don't think, because we were twins, but just something that sisters do. People just got used to seeing us together, so they never had to figure out which one they were talking to. Understand, so far?"

"Yes. I think the two of you are closer than most siblings I know. Even Dillon is very close to you two. I'm assuming you leaned on each other a great deal when you were growing up." She told him they were all they had, despite having parents. "That's sad that the two people that were supposed to love you didn't do a very good job of getting to know you. Go on. Tell me what you need to."

"Thank you." She got up again, walking to the new windows to look at the back yard. Cole could tell he was going to have to have the faeries spruce it up a little bit before the weather turned again. "We were headed into town with Mom to do some school shopping. We had just turned twelve, and to us, that was such a big deal. In fact, we were already telling people we were going to be thirteen soon. That started the day after our birthday."

She laughed a little but didn't come back to the table. Instead, she stared out at the back yard and commented on it needing someone to fix it up. As soon as the words were out of her mouth, Watson was moving to the group of faeries. Cole would bet anything before she finished her tale; the yard would be beautiful.

"Mom would get sidetracked when we were with her. It never occurred to either of us, I don't think that she was a terrible person for leaving two young girls alone in a large department store. So we made our way to the girl's department but got caught up in the display for the older kid's section." Ryan laughed but didn't say what she found funny. When she turned toward him, he could see that the faeries were indeed working in the yard. "We never dressed alike. Well, we might have as babies, but I don't remember seeing any pictures of us when we were infants, so I have no way of knowing. Rylie and I grabbed an armload of clothing and headed to the dressing room."

He wasn't sure he wanted to hear the rest. Cole had to calm his dragon several times while she stood there. The tears rolling down her cheeks had him wanting to grab her up and take her away from whatever was bothering her. But he also knew that on some level, he needed to hear what she had to tell him.

Chapter 4

Closing her eyes to remember, she could see the man standing there as if it were happening all over again. However, when strong arms wrapped around her, lifting her up from the floor, she leaned her head into Cole's chest and listened to his heart beating, beating harder due to his anger, which wasn't aimed at her. Ryan didn't know why she understood that, but she did.

"We entered the changing room, knowing full well that if anything we got didn't fit, we'd not be able to bring it back. Mom would take us there, get what we handed her, and then we'd be done until the next school year." She let out a long breath as she continued. "The door to the little area closed behind us. Neither of us took any notice of it, as we were excited to be able to do this on our own. It wasn't until we heard the door locking that we turned and saw him standing there."

She thought about all the things that had been done to them. More of the things that might well have happened to them had either of them been alone in the tiny changing room. The things the man had threatened them with clung in her mind every time she thought of that day and the weeks of recuperating later. Holding Cole's hand, she continued.

"He was naked. He also had a gun. Pointing it at us, he told us to take off our clothes. 'Take everything off,' he said several times." She told how they'd been too slow for the man. That he'd hit Rylie with the butt of the gun and then ripped her things from her. "He said we were going to fix him up. Since we were only kids, we didn't have any idea what he was talking about. But he was excited. His cock wasn't large, but it was hard. As soon as he touched Rylie with his hand, he came all over her."

"Where was your mother at this time?" Ryan said they didn't know until later, but she'd left them there in favor of going home. "She just decided that two twelve-year-old children were going to be fine at the store alone? Christ."

"It wasn't the first time she'd done something like that. We didn't have anything like a cell phone either. As much as I'd like to say it was the last time, it wasn't." Letting out a slow breath, she told Cole about the man. "He masturbated over us several times while he had us locked in the tiny rooms. By then, he'd tied Rylie to the door to one of the rooms. I think it was to keep me in line. But as he started to hit Rylie several times, I started to hit back. It was then that he decided he wanted sex." She thought about what she'd done next. Told Cole of the things he'd done to them when he raped them both. It wasn't as hard to tell him as she thought it might have been. However, she could feel his anger as it got stronger and stronger. Stopping, she looked at him. "There isn't any reason for you to be angry, Cole. Really. It happened a long time ago. And even though it still haunts us both, we've been able to, for the most part, put it behind us."

"Perhaps you have—a little at least. But for me, I want to kill the fucker right now. Even if he is dead, I want to find him, dig him up, then kill him in ways that would make me feel so much better." He kissed her on the nose, a place she was suddenly finding erotic. "Go on now. Tell me the rest so I can feel better."

"I think we were in the room for a few hours. When we were able to get away, the store had long since closed, and it was dark outside. Neither of us had a cell phone, so we found one in the billing department and called the police." He asked what had happened to the man. "He is dead."

"You killed him." She nodded and closed her eyes. "How? Did you kill him with his own gun, Ryan?"

"No. It wasn't even real. The gun, I mean. It was a water pistol." She looked at him and saw something there that not even her own mother had displayed. Compassion. Love, and even understanding. Neither of her parents had ever understood any of their children. "I took one of the hangers that was in the room with us and beat him with it. I couldn't stop. Rylie was hurting badly by then because of me fighting him back. So was I, but I was more angry than in pain. I hit him in the throat with the hanger crook and ripped his throat out."

"Good for you." Ryan asked him if he'd heard what she'd just said. "I did. You saved the two of you by killing a bastard. I'm sure that everyone thought you did a wonderful thing in killing him."

"No. Some did. The police, especially. They were so happy we were both all right that they visited us in the hospital daily. Our parents didn't, however. They were embarrassed that we'd called the police before calling them. You see, the police found us in the store naked and covered from our head to our feet in ejaculation and blood. Mom didn't speak to us for months afterwards. Dad grounded us for our part in a man's death." Cole told her that he was glad and proud of her for killing the man. "We didn't get our names in the paper. However, they did say that we were twins. It didn't take much to figure out it was us. People were calling our parents and telling them what a wonderful thing we'd done. That only made matters worse. Right up until the day they were killed, they never forgave us for doing what we'd done."

Standing up, Cole held her in his arms. When he swung her around, laughing like a loon, she asked him what he thought was so funny. After kissing her, making her feel like something special and fragile, he put his forehead to hers and smiled.

"You not only saved your sister but me as well. Don't you see? Had you not done what you did, then we would never have met. Because I know that he would have killed you, both of you, so he'd be able to do what he'd done again and again." She asked him how he knew. "Because, my dearest love, he was practiced at what he'd done in the first place. He knew where to hide. How long he would have been able to keep you. No one checked those areas to see if anyone was still in the store when it closed. He knew that. Do you know his name?"

She told him. "What do you think you're going to do with his name? I told you he was dead. I killed him." He kissed her again, briefly this time. She stared at him as his smile got larger and larger. "You're scaring me right now. What are you thinking about?"

"He's dead." She nodded, sure that he'd had a stroke or something the way he kept dancing around the room. "I'm having Connor see if he can find him. He just told me that he hasn't moved on. Now we're going to get the real scoop on what his plans had been for the two of you. Also, find out if he'd been doing this for some time. I believe he had been. Connor is speaking to him right now."

She felt someone touch her mind. It was Connor. When he asked her to hang on for just a moment, she could feel another person there. It was sort of like a party-line when Connor asked Cole if he was there yet.

"I am. Tell her what you were able to find out about the man." Connor told her that the man hadn't moved on because he was terrified of where he'd end up. "Is that usual?"

For his type of person, yes. He had killed fourteen other children with the scam he was playing while alive. No one had been able to catch him because they didn't know where he was going to strike next. Each time he'd raped them, he slit their throats. There were no witnesses to lay blame at his feet until the two of you. You and your sister getting out, he told me, was his greatest failure. Just so you know, I'm sending him on. It's time he paid for his crimes. Cole asked about the other children. *They weren't twins if that is what you mean. He hadn't ever taken two people back to his hiding places in different stores across the tri-state area. However, with you, Ryan. Had it not been for you and your sister killing him, he said that he'd have gone on doing what he'd done because it was fun for him. His thinking is that you and Rylie should have been hurt more before he tried to end your lives. He's pissed off that his first time having two was the most fun but also ended his life. He is one sick fucker. Honey, I'm so proud of you for this. For not just killing this monster, but telling Cole about it so I could move him on. He will never bother anyone ever again.*

"I thought with him being dead, that was obvious." Conner explained. "I didn't know he could still cause trouble after death. I didn't know anything but that dead was dead. Thank you for telling me. I appreciate it more than I can explain."

After Connor left their minds, she hadn't any idea what that would have been called, she got up and wandered around the house again. Cole didn't follow her. Ryan was glad for it. She needed this time. Alone. After spilling out the story and knowing that at least two people thought she and Rylie had done well for themselves, she stood in front of the windowed doors that led to what she thought was a backyard paradise.

"'Tis a solarium, my lady." She asked him what that meant. Ryan thought it was a greenhouse, but Watson told her that since it wasn't one for planting, but having plants, the humans had called it a solarium. "I believe it a place where you can go and be warm around beautiful plants while you think on your day. I have seen, in my time, where ladies of the house would come to places like this to write letters. Entertain guests while having tea. Things that they knew would show off what they'd been able to keep growing in such harsh winters." Watson laughed.

"Why do you think that is so funny? I'd think this would be just the place for you to hang out too." He told her that he had. "Then, why do you laugh? I could use a good giggle myself, I think."

"'Tis only that the ladies of the house would have nothing to do with such things, but they would show it off as if they'd had their hands dirty." He looked at her. "I think you'd be out here, digging in the earth, however. You look to be a woman who would not depend on others for the beauty surrounding you. Is that right?"

"I've never done it. Planted anything, I mean. I'm sure as a child, I played outdoors. However, you're right. I could be depended on to do my fair share of work." Ryan looked at Watson when he landed on her hand she'd put out for him. "I would never ask anyone to do anything I'd not do myself. That would include staff and you. You're going to be very good for me, aren't you, Watson? I mean, just to have a person around that I can bounce ideas off of."

"You think of me as a person?" She knew the moment Cole had joined them in the room. "My lord, she thinks I am equal to her as a person. My heart right now is so large I think I'm to burst with it. A person. Did you hear that? I'm a person."

When Watson flew away, she turned and looked at Cole. He was still tracking the little man as he flew around the top of the room they were in. She could see that there were several others like Watson up there with him. She asked him what Watson had meant by being proud to be a person.

"Most would think of him only as a way to get things done. Not an equal, as you had called him by saying he was a person. Faeries are a very shy yet vain group of beings. For months now, the other faeries will hear of nothing else from him but that you called him a person. I'm sure the story will get larger with each telling. It may well be that you've fallen in love with him and will only call on him to do things for you that even I cannot do." Ryan told Cole she was sorry. "No, don't be. It's harmless. The others will know that I'd die for you and that while Watson is a good faerie for you, he will never be my equal."

"Thank you. I think." She looked around the room they were standing in. "He told me this room was a place for the lady of the house to entertain. I don't know how much of that I'd be doing. I don't care for tea. Sitting around on my ass to talk to others isn't really that much fun. Nor do I think having a computer out here to work would do much good for me. I'd be distracted all the time, wondering what the flowers are blooming into that I can explore. I don't want to get rid of the area, but I don't see me using it as a place to unwind either."

"I don't know. I can see you coming here to perhaps get some sort of poison to put in my stew should I piss you off. I don't doubt there will be times when I will get on your last nerve." She wasn't sure if he was joking or not until he laughed. "I have been known to be a tad bit stubborn about things. Things that get my health into jeopardy. I was lain low not too long ago when I tried to take on more than I should have. I know better now."

"I should hope so. Now that I'm used to having you around, I'd rather not have to figure out how to be without you." Ryan turned and looked at Cole. "There are times when I think you're insane for wanting to be around me. Then others, I try to figure out why I need you in my life so badly. Those are easier to figure out than why you want to be around me."

"I love you, that's why." She stared at him, his eyes telling her that he really did believe he loved her. "I do, Ryan. So very much so. I would do anything for you, but I won't. You've pointed out that can be dangerous to myself, but I would if you'd allow it."

"I don't know what I want from you." She looked around, then back at him. "I would very much like to live here with you if you're sure. And all that entails. I mean sleeping with you, in case you didn't understand."

Cole pulled her tightly to his body. Not so tight that she felt trapped, but she did feel his erection. Neither of them said anything about sex when he pulled away. Taking her hand into his, they moved through the rest of the house, making changes with the help of the faeries as they went.

To say that she was confused was an understatement. Did he not want her to live here? Was he appalled by her story? She supposed time would tell. As they exited the house, Watson told her he'd have the house ready when they returned. That he'd meet her later. Ryan had completely forgotten that they were leaving tonight to go to the trial of Sandra.

~*~

Cole enjoyed the company of the others. When they went out to dinner as a group, he knew full well that the staff, including the cooks, would be well tipped. Their group was loud, friendly, as well as fun. Even when things were going to be serious or have to be taken care of, they would find some humor in what they were up to, and that made dealing with things much easier. At least it was for him.

Cole did keep an eye on Dillon and Rylie. She was a timid little thing, while Dillon tried his best to be a part of the things going on around him. He was never shut down, but Cole could tell that Dillon didn't want to interrupt anyone when they were speaking. As was the habit of the group, they'd cut a person off when they had something else to impart to whatever you were saying. Dillon was intimidated by that. He was, however, getting used to it or realizing that he had to be one of them if he ever expected to be able to say anything at the table.

He noticed that Ryan didn't have any trouble fitting in with them. Cole supposed that was in part why she was his mate — that she could and did give as good as she got. It made him laugh out loud when she took one of them to task, especially when she would tell Devon that he was full of shit. The big dragon didn't know how to take her being up in his face.

After dinner, they hung around a little longer than he'd thought they would. It wasn't until the attorney that was taking the case for Dillon showed up that he understood. He told them what he knew, which was a great deal, thanks mostly to the other women of the group. They were not only well connected with what they were into, but a few of them weren't opposed to calling a stranger and getting what they wanted from them.

Even his own mate had the ear to the president. Not that she wanted it, but she had it. He'd been calling the house a few times a week to speak to Ryan. He wasn't sure she was unhappy about the input she could give him, but she was getting sick of telling him that she no longer wanted to work for him. It hadn't set well with the man. Thanks to him, they had some information that Cole doubted they would have gotten from anywhere else.

"The satellite clearly shows that your wife was driving the car that hit your parents. That's all we have; unfortunately, just her getting out of the car and going to the other car. But it's more than enough, I think, to show that she was a part of the death of the two of them. That, along with the insurance policy she took out on them, shows premeditation." Ryan asked what would happen to her. "That's why I had hoped to talk to the three of you tonight. I need for Dillon, as we talked about before, to tell the courts that he no longer wishes to press charges against his wife in the matter where she tried to kill him. At least at this time. You must remember to say that, young man. Otherwise, we can't go back and visit that if this other doesn't pan out. I don't foresee any issues with that, but you never know what is going to happen when there are crowds of people around."

Dillon agreed, and then he told Rylie and Ryan what their part in this would be. It was going to be tricky, Cole thought, to time things just the way the lawyer wanted them to, but in the end, it would make sure that Sandra was kept in jail for a very long time. That was what they wanted, while the others wanted her dead.

Going back to the hotel, he was glad he'd gotten separate rooms from Ryan. She was going to spend some time with her brother and sister. He knew they were close, and the only way they'd make this work for their brother was to convince him that it would. However, before going into the room, the three of them were sharing, she came to him.

"I'm in love with you." He smiled at her, unsure what she was going to say next. That was something he'd learned about her tonight—she wasn't nearly finished telling you something when she paused a little bit. "I'm not sure about tomorrow nor what happens years from now. But I do know that I want to spend the rest of whatever time we have being immortal living with you and loving you more daily."

"Will you marry me?" She asked him if that was necessary. "It is to me. While I can understand not wanting a ceremony, I would like to have that we're married filed in the courthouse. In later years, it will help with us changing names around should that become necessary."

"Because you're around forever." He nodded, pulling her into his arms, no longer able to resist having her close enough to touch. "Okay. I don't have any problem with that. However, I would like for you to set up a trip if you'd not mind. I want to get away. To get out of my comfort zone and travel for a while. Would that be all right with you?"

"It would. Very much so." She nodded. Kissing him, pulling him to her, had his cock stretching in his pants so much that he had to adjust himself or be in more pain than he'd been in a while. When she grinned at him, he laughed. "How on this earth did I go for so long thinking that a mate would be something that would tie me down?"

"I don't know. But when you do figure it out, let me know. I have been wondering the same thing." She started to pull away but turned back to him. "I don't have much, but I have money. I'd like to, if you don't mind, set something up with it to give my brother and sister some starting money. Kelly told me they'd be around forever as well."

"They will, and we have more than enough money to help with whatever adventures they'd like to start out with. I do believe Dillon has accepted the job with working for our family as an investment broker. Your sister, what is it she likes to get into?" Ryan told him.

"Doctorate in Psychology? Well, I'm not sure I have much need for that right now, but I'm sure if we put our heads together, we can get her happy too. She's very shy. Is it to do with the man?"

"No. She's always been shy. To hear her tell it, she had to be so that people would know it was me when trouble started. I don't think I was that bad, but it has worked for her for a long time. Also, she was always putting together things. Organizing events for the school or whatever people needed. She's very good at that and comes out of her shell when she gets going." Cole told her he could use someone like that. "Good. You talk to her. I'm going to be thinking of ways to jump your bones."

With that parting statement, she left him there. It wasn't until Faith closed his mouth that he realized he was standing there with it hanging open. Looking at the little faerie he'd been with since he was a little dragon, he saw her smiling at him.

"I would like to talk to you, sir." He told her that he needed a moment. "Yes. But 'tis important."

"All right, my dear. What is it that is so important that I can't feel good about my mate loving me?" She told him, of course, she loved him. "Yes, well, she's only just said the words. I was basking in them when you rudely interrupted me."

"You are very strange. I think there is a mate for her sister." That did get his attention. "I thought for a little while that you were wrong in Lady Ryan being your mate. But then I saw that it was her sister the man was staring at."

"Are you sure it's a mate and not just someone trying to get at her?" Faith told him she was sure of his intentions. "Then why is he not claiming her? Do you know what his reason would be for waiting?"

"He is...I'm not sure what it is called. But he is not perfect." Cole entered his room before they drew attention to themselves. He asked her to explain. "He is part werewolf. Not wolf, my lord, but the 'were' sort. The other part of him I do not know at all. But he thinks of himself as imperfect and cannot bring himself to claim such a beauty. I thought he was having trouble with telling the two apart. But that doesn't seem to be an issue. He knows which is which. I sometimes do not, but he does. As do you, now that I think on it."

"It's because she calls to me. This man. Do you know anything about him? His name would be nice to know so I can have him looked into." She told him what she knew of him—nothing helpful, but he did know more than he had before. "He owns part of this establishment, so he must have money, wouldn't you think? Not that it's necessary to have yourself set up like we are, but it would be better, don't you think?"

"I know only that he is part owner here. That he is a half breed of a race I thought long since gone." Cole asked her if she thought he'd be up for a talk. "I can ask him. He knows of me and that I'm here. He is also aware of the reason we're here. I was concerned about that, but as it is in the newspaper, I didn't think he was spying on anyone. What do you think we should tell Lady Ryan?"

"I have no idea. Should we wait for a move on his part?" She said she was not going to give him advice for his mate. "Are you by chance afraid of Lady Ryan?"

"I am, my lord. We all are." When she shivered then sat down on the pillow of his bed, he could see that she really was concerned about Ryan. "She has never harmed me. Nor has she spoken to me as you do when you are out of your head with something bothering you. But there is something about her, a strength I cannot name just yet, that frightens me, as well as the other faeries. She has a magic about her that doesn't match anything you have. It's not dark, but it isn't wholly white either."

He'd have to think on that. Right now, he was more concerned with William Spencer. What did he know about them? Better yet, what was his reasoning for not approaching Rylie when he had to be aware of what they were? Or did he?

Cole knew that having Bryce around them would deter anyone or anything from coming around that would cause them harm. The grand witch would be able to perhaps not kill whatever came at them, but she could put them in a world of hurt. Cole also bet that she'd blanket what she considered her family with something to hide what they actually were. The way they were protective of one another, himself included, he'd also bet they had more than just the faeries keeping them safe.

As he laid down on his bed, he thought of all the people that had been in the dining room with them this evening. More than just help, he wondered now. Laughing as he rolled to his side, stripping off his clothing as he did so, he also thought he'd have to have a talk with the younger woman. Cole could and would lend her whatever she needed in the way of strength when she needed it for this.

"My lord, there is something else I just remembered. The woman in the jail cell, she is not right in the head. I know you must be aware of that, but I wanted to tell you that the faeries watching her think she is very evil as well." He turned and asked her what she had found out. "She can call to her black magic to make those around her do what she wishes."

That was something he hadn't thought of—Sandra being able to get out of what was going to happen in the morning. Reaching out to Noah to ask if he could speak to his wife for a few moments, he only got a tingling of a warning before their images appeared in front of them. The two of them looked as if they were having a good time eating popcorn and watching a movie. He told them what he'd only just found out.

"Thank you for that." When Bryce laughed, Cole pulled his blankets up more over his chest. "I will take care of this when we arrive. The faeries you have watching her—did you know that I have a few there as well?"

When Faith shook her head, he told Bryce he'd not been aware. "I didn't want anything to get past us, as this is my family now. Anything that happens to anyone here will mean the death of the woman." Bryce assured him that she wouldn't be a problem. "You're that sure? That positive that the outcome will make them all safe?"

"Even if the outcome does not go in our favor, Cole, I swear to you that she will no longer be a problem for anyone." He nodded. There wasn't anything better that he could have asked from someone. "I do thank you for the information. Also, if your faerie does have any luck finding mine, I would appreciate it. They've been missing since the day after I sent them there."

"I will go and search for them now, my lady Grand Witch." When Faith left them, he looked at Noah when he said his name.

"Keep your loved ones close tomorrow, my friend. While we cannot figure out the way things are going to go with the judge, we do know there will be magic. I wouldn't want to be Sandra tomorrow if things go according to plan. Or for that matter, even if they don't."

Once their connection was closed, he laid back on his bed. Instead of lying there, waiting on the sun to rise, he got up and dressed. He needed to do something. Making sure that his sister-in-law was safe seemed like a good distraction for him.

As soon as he was put in touch with the man, he

decided to check out the bar that was still open. Not that he could get drunk. However, Cole did enjoy a nice glass or two of wine on occasion. He would have to remember to have his collection brought here. Some of the wines he had were priceless.

As soon as William came to meet him, Cole felt better about a great many things.

Chapter 5

The courtroom was packed. Dillon wasn't sure if it all had to do with Sandra or not until he heard a couple of people talking about her. Neighbors, he figured, when they spoke about how she wasn't mowing her lawn before the house was burnt to the ground. They seemed to know that she'd had some start the fire too. Also, he heard she had been tossing her trash into their yards over the years. She'd been causing more than just trouble with him, it appeared. A lot of people around here wanted her to get her comeuppance. He surely hoped today was the day that she got it. He wanted an end to this, and her, in the worst sort of way.

Even though he'd been granted a divorce immediately after filing for one, he was still afraid to be near her. Fear? No, it wasn't that. It was something more akin to being sickened by her. She'd killed his parents. They weren't the best parents by any stretch of the imagination, but they had been his.

Dillon would be forever grateful to Devon and the rest of the men for showing him how the magic he'd been given would keep him safe. Also, and this was something he tried very hard not to get too excited about, he could kill Sandra if she were to attack him. Twice now since coming here, he'd had thoughts of how he'd make her suffer should she try something with any of them. But he also knew he wasn't the type of person that would kill simply because he could.

"Are you ready for this?" He told Ryan he'd never been so ready for something. "Don't lie to me, Dillon. I need to know you're not going to cut bait and run from her. You remember what Cole told you. You have to show her you're not terrified of her anymore. I know I have to work on that as well, but I do feel much better about being here."

"To be honest with you, big sister, I'm not sure how I feel about her. Nothing good, I can tell you that. She's a monster and needs to be put away. However, what scares me more than anything is what Bryce told us at breakfast. What if she does try to use some magic, and it gets by Bryce?" Ryan laughed and told him she didn't think much got by any of them. "Yes, well, I guess you're right about that. I do have a question for you. A change of subject, if you will. How rich do you think these people are? I mean, they don't act like I thought rich people do.

I'm sure they have millions."

"Billions." Dillon started to laugh, but Ryan only stared at him. "Billions upon billions. Cole told me they don't even bother putting money in bank accounts anymore. There is just too much of it to expect a bank to be able to cover if something happened. Not that it would hurt any of them, or us for that matter if the bank was robbed. They have that much."

He looked at the man who'd told him yesterday that he was in love with Ryan. Cole told him he was his brother. Not in-law, he told him, but his brother. And that whatever he had, so would Dillon. It had taken Dillon most of the next day to realize that Cole meant just what he said, especially after showing him the houses he wanted Dillon to choose from. Several big homes that would put the one he'd shared with Sandra to shame. Rylie had been treated the same way.

"My home, it's not far from yours, did you know that?" Ryan said she did and was glad that Rylie was going to be close to them too. "I tried to tell Cole that I had enough money coming in that I didn't need for him to give me a home, but he just shrugged me off. If it were possible for me to have picked someone for you to love, Ryan, it would have been him. Cole is perfect for you. He's about the nicest man I've ever known. Even with the three of us being so close, he doesn't get all pissy when we're together. I have never felt like he wished us gone when we're together. It's like he is happy for you."

"He is. He told me that whatever made me happy, makes him happy."

Dillon hugged his sister and turned when the bailiff came into the room, telling them to stand. Cole sat down on the other side of Ryan when they were seated again. Rylie was on Dillon's other side. The four of them together made Dillon feel like he could take on the world and come out on top.

Then Sandra came out of the side door and stood there staring at him.

"She's going down, little brother. You mark my words. She won't hurt you again."

Sandra didn't look a thing like he had hoped she would. Her hair was neat and pulled back from her face. The clothing she had on was a nice outfit that he knew she'd worn before. Where she'd gotten it, Dillon didn't know, but she looked cleaned up and polished like she did every time they were going someplace. But behind the façade, he knew, was a terrible person. Someone that would and *had* killed to get what she wanted.

The judge was handed a few files. In them, Dillon knew, was his divorce paperwork, as well as copies of the insurance policies that had been taken out on his parents. For whatever reason, Sandra had put his name on the beneficiary page along with her own. Noah told him that she wanted it to look good, but he had a feeling that Sandra had expected him to be dead when it came to cashing it in. He was sure she hadn't expected to be caught.

Sometimes the family's honesty was a bit much. Dillon had to laugh, however. He'd never met a more generous group. Not just with what they had, but what they knew as well. Dillon was enjoying his time speaking to Susanna too. She was a wealth of information.

"Mr. Cord?" Dillon stood up and said that was him. The judge nodded and smiled at him. "It is my understanding that you have something to say before we begin?"

"Yes, sir. It is my desire that I do not press charges against my ex-wife, Sandra Cord, at this time. I may at a later date. I know I have an additional thirty days should I change my mind, but for now, I'm not going to do that."

Judge Peterson nodded and smiled again. Before Dillon could say the rest of what he wanted to say, the judge looked at Sandra.

"Well, it seems to be your lucky day, Ms. Cord. Bailiff, please remove the handcuffs from her." When she was released, just as they'd planned, his sisters stood up and asked to speak to the judge. "Of course you may. Please state your full name as well as your relationship with Mr. Cord there."

Ryan spoke first. "My name is Doctor Ryan Jamerson, Lady of Jamerson Castle, Duchess of Mink. I have a Doctor of Forensic Psychology. Also, I'm the older sister of Doctor Dillon Cord."

He'd forgotten that Ryan was a duchess. Dillon had

to stifle a laugh when his sister called herself a lady. He knew her far better than most did, and he had never considered his sister a lady at all. However, it was the doctor that had thrown him for a moment. Ryan had gone to college to become a doctor of forensic pathology. Then his other sister spoke.

"My name is Doctor Rylie Cord, Doctor of Psychology, older sister to Doctor Dillon Cord, Doctor of Finance." Judge Peterson said that their family must be proud of them. "I don't know, sir. They were murdered a few months ago. That's why we're here. It has been shown to us that Sandra Cord murdered them for the gain of an insurance policy. The three of us would like to press those charges against her at this time."

No one moved in the courtroom. He was sure they were as stunned as they'd been when they were told about the murders. The bailiff, still in the process of uncuffing Sandra, just stared at the judge with his mouth open. Sandra, however, had plenty to say when no one moved to release her.

"What are you talking about? I demand that you take that back. You were forever jealous of me, Rylie Cord. And now here you are making up lies to keep me away from your family." Sandra laughed. "Well, I have news for you, little girl. I want nothing to do with any of you. So what? I took out a policy on your parents. They were old, and how the hell was I supposed to know they'd be killed by *a drunk driver*." Sandra had screamed out the last part.

"Ms. Cord, this is quite a leap from her trying to murder Mr. Cord here to murdering your parents. It was my understanding that—" Sandra was still going on about how they were just trying to keep her from the money. That they had nothing on her but their hatred of her for thinking ahead. "Will you please shut your trap? My goodness, you can go on about things, can't you? Hush now while I try my best to figure this out. Now. Ms. Cord. You know that without some sort of proof of this allegation, then I'm going to have to turn you down for this."

"I have proof, Your Honor."

Their attorney stood up and called for help. As the projector was being set up, Dillon felt something touch him. It wasn't painful. He looked around to see who might be doing it.

Sandra was staring at him. Her mouth was moving, and he could see her fingers, which were still behind her, moving as well. It wasn't until Bryce came to stand next to him that he was sure it was magic. The laughter coming from Bryce had him turning to look at her. But it was the movement—or in this case, the lack of movement—that caught his eye.

No one was moving. The projector that was being brought into the courtroom was still a few inches from the table. The judge was in mid-word when whatever it was caught him. It wasn't a good look for the older gentleman, not the way his face was pinched up. There were others caught in mid-movement too. Dillon looked at his sisters when they turned to look at Bryce.

"I've done this, yes." He asked her what it was that she'd done. "No one will be aware of this pause in their work here. But I wanted to talk to you about Sandra. She's violating all the laws of our kind. And even though she isn't a witch like I am, her using the black magic to have things turn in her way lets me get to deal with her. I had hoped she would try something like this."

"No magic should be used for the betterment of yourself." Bryce nodded at him. "With working for you guys, I was given some books I could use to know the way things work. She is going to be dealt with by you for trying to use magic on us."

"No. Just on you. Even though you are the one she was working on, it was what the outcome would have been should I not have been warned about her magic. She was going to have you take the gun from the bailiff there and kill your sisters, then yourself. She'd have left here without anyone being the wiser when you three were dead."

Bryce moved to stand in front of Sandra. When she snapped her fingers, Sandra continued doing whatever it was she'd been working on when the room stopped moving.

"Hello, Sandra Elizabeth Markum Cord. Do you know who I am?"

"No. And I don't know if you realize this or not, but I really couldn't care at all." Sandra seemed to realize the same thing he'd noticed. "What the hell is going on in here? Did you do this? For me? Well, aren't you the best thing that's happened to me in a while. Thanks."

"This was done by me, yes, but it was because of you, not for you. I'm Bryce Farley, Grand Witch to all magic, black or white. You were given the rules of your kind when you decided to take this pathway into magic, were you not?" Sandra asked her what she had to pay to get out of this. "I'm afraid it's not that easy, Sandra Elizabeth Markum Cord. You see, when you murdered those two people, you did so with magic. Another gain for yourself. Hurting your husband, you used magic to put him into a deeper sleep so you could do the most damage possible before he was able to call the police. There are other things, other deaths too, that can be attributed to your usage of black magic."

"Whatever the fine is, I'm willing to pay it. I plead guilty. Whatever it takes to get you out of my face." Sandra looked back at him. "He was nothing to me, but a means to get more money. I'd be out of this shit right here if it wasn't for Dillon and his nosey assed sisters. Christ, when I think of all the shit, I had to endure while married to him. I think I should just be let off with this as a warning. Come on. You've been around him. You know what I'm talking about."

"I don't, actually. What I've come to figure out

about Dillon is that he's a nice man. An honorable man too. Being married to you must have taken a great deal from him. Because all I can see with him is him growing stronger daily and becoming the man he might well have been for you had you given him a slight chance." Bryce laughed and turned to wink at him before she looked at Sandra again. "I will take your magic now."

Sandra staggered and would have fallen but for the table beside her. Dillon didn't know what had happened, but he thought it was just what Bryce had said—she'd taken her magic. When she started screaming for Bryce to stop, Dillon looked at Sandra.

"Oh my god. What the hell is that?" He sat down— there wasn't any strength in his legs to hold him up. Even as he watched his ex-wife, never taking his eyes from her, he still had trouble making his mind see what was right in front of him. "Christ. I'm going to be sick."

Rushing out of the room, he heard the screams of the others. He knew the room was now resuming what they'd been doing before Bryce had stepped in. Dillon knew for as long as he lived, he'd never be able to think about Sandra without seeing the lasting image of her dying in the courtroom.

~*~

Ryan was sitting out on the deck when he returned home. Being called away right now was the last thing he'd wanted to happen. But Ryan assured him that she was going to be fine and told him to go. It had been one of the hardest things he'd ever done.

"Do you suppose she knew what would happen when she took the magic away from her?" He hadn't realized she'd noticed him at the doorway until then. "I mean, it was very ugly and nasty. Do you think Bryce was aware that Sandra was older, much older than she looked when Dillon married her?"

"I would think she would. Bryce knows her magic better than anyone I've ever encountered." Cole sat down on the chair beside her. Picking her up, he put her on his lap. "I needed to hold you. I hope you don't mind."

"No. I was going to ask you for a hug anyway. It's been a strange couple of days." He'd bet. "The attorney's office called this morning and said that Sandra's parents are dead as well. I think Sandra was keeping them alive all this time so she could use them. Bryce said she'd only bring them out of the deep sleep they were in when she needed them for something. Since she wasn't in the will, keeping them alive and making them support her was the only way she could get money from them. Sandra was one sick fucker if you ask me."

"I think you're about as right in your explanation as anyone else. How is Dillon? I know he was still upset when we got back here. I thought he was pissed off at Bryce, but he assured me it wasn't her." Ryan told him what she knew. "I can see that. I think I'd be pissed at myself, too, if I was tricked into a marriage. But it wasn't his fault. He knows that, doesn't he?"

"Mentally, I think he does, but his heart is really hurting. I don't even think it's because she betrayed him for so long. He seemed to be more pissed that he was being bamboozled into shit he didn't know about." Cole needed to tell Ryan something, but he wasn't sure she was ready for it yet. "Tell me."

"What?" She told him that he'd been hemming and hawing around for two days now about something. "You, my dear mate, have been hanging around Susanna for far too long. Hemming and hawing? But yes, I do have something to tell you. It's about your sister. Her mate is here."

She turned and looked at him so quickly he nearly dropped her. Instead of telling her what he'd found out, he started at the beginning, when Faith had figured it out at the hotel, they'd been in a few days ago.

"I've met with him. He's a nice man. His name is William Spencer. He and his partner, his brother, actually, have a lot of businesses they're running. Wealthy. Smart too. And he's part werewolf and fae." She asked him what the difference was between a were and a wolf. "William believes that he and his brother are the last of their kind. You know what a fae is, I'm assuming. A werewolf is a wolf that walks upright. There are other differences as well, but that's the most important one. He can shift all or part of his body, depending on what he is doing. His strength is legendary too. When I talked with his brother Jacob, he told me that they've been around for about as long as we have. Old as well as powerful men, both of them are. William said he'd wait to hear from me before he went to talk to her. Also, he's willing to relocate to here so that Rylie can see her family whenever she wishes."

"How do you know he's a good man? I mean, he could be just like the creatures we see in movies and is waiting around to kill her in her sleep." Cole just looked at her. "Okay, I know he can't hurt her. I'm assuming he can't anyway. Do you think that Rylie will be safe with him? That she'll fall in love with him like the rest of us have with our mates?"

"I do. While we were talking, I had Devon look into him for me. Not only is he an upstanding man, but he's also like us in that he donates a great deal of his personal time and money in order to see those around him, the ones that make a start for themselves, are able to move up in the world too." She laid her head back on his chest, and he laughed a little. "You're either so mad at me that you don't know what to say, or you're plotting my death. Which is it so that I can be prepared."

"Neither. I was actually thinking how happy Rylie will be. She needs someone in her life." Cole didn't say anything but waited for her to finish. "I don't suppose you found anyone for Dillon, did you? I mean, if anyone deserves a second chance at life, it would be him. I want him to be the happiest of all of us."

"Nothing that I'm aware of." He turned her on his lap, so she faced the woods. "If you look out beyond the pool house, you'll be able to see William now. He's been coming by here for the last several days to check on your sister. He would also like to speak to you and Dillon. I believe he is going to prove to the two of you that he can take care of your sister very well."

"So long as he makes her laugh once in a while, I'll be thrilled with him." She stood up and waved the man toward them. "I'm going to go in and call my sister. I know I can do that mind thing, but I think this is something that needs to be said to her. Also, I'm going to send Dillon out. He's packing his things up to move into the home you guys fixed up for him."

She went into the house but came back out before William got to the deck. Cole did have a moment of worry when she turned to him. Standing up, he was going to defend her to the death if she didn't like or didn't want William around her sister.

"I know this is for the best. I'm happy for my sister. But the more you find to do, the longer it's going to take for us to be in our big bed having fun."

Cole stared at the door that she went back through. When William asked him if he was all right, Cole laughed.

"Women are the most wonderful beings in the world, I think. However, they can turn a person, even a full grown dragon, on his ear without much in the way of effort." William joined him in laugher. "She's sending her brother out now. Also calling her sister. Rylie went into town today to see if she could find a place to hang her shingle. She's decided she can be more useful as a psychologist than she can anything else. You will allow her to work, won't you?"

"I would have no say in what she does at all. It is her mind and body. Anything she wishes will be my goal to make happen for her." Cole told William what Ryan had told him about being so agreeable all the time. "Yes. I can see that. To be honest with you, Cole, I know very little about women. Are they as scary as they seem to be?"

"Much more so." Dillon put out his hand when he answered William. "You hurt my sister, and your brother will be the last one of your kind. She's been through a great deal, and I won't have anyone, not any creature, harm my family. And that would include this one."

"I would allow you to kill me if I were to hurt such a beauty as your sister." When they sat down, Cole had a feeling they were sizing each other up. He was all for that. William looked at him before too much time had passed and smiled at him. "I believe I could learn a great deal from this family about keeping their loved ones safe."

They talked between the three of them for about an hour. When Ryan came out to tell them she was going to get her sister, William introduced himself to her. As soon as she shook his hand, the power jolt to his own system startled him. Looking at William, he seemed just as surprised by the magical transfer.

"I'm not Rylie." William told her he knew that, as did

his beast. "You'd be better off if you didn't call your other half a beast until she meets you both. If you understand that I'm not your mate, what was the transfer of magic? I'm assuming that is what it was."

"I don't know for sure what you got, but Dillon did as well. He didn't mention it, and I was surprised by that as well. He must, in his own right, be— You were married to the woman that died of unexplained causes, weren't you?" Dillon asked if he meant Sandra, and when William said that was her, he nodded. "She wasn't really a witch, but she did use black magic for her own personal use. If so, that explains why you didn't feel or feel well the magic I gave you. You have hers."

"I don't want her black magic." William told him that it was no longer black, but as pure as the snow on the ground in January. "Why would I get it? I thought you had to kill a witch to gain her powers."

"Ah, but you did kill her, young Dillon. When you and your sisters came together to see to her getting her just punishment, you made her death possible. Don't you see?" Dillon looked at him, and Cole told him he had no idea but that Bryce would be the one to ask. "So many different kinds of magic in one family. It is scary yet comforting, don't you think? I would say that besides being the wealthiest family in the world, you are far and away the most magical as well. I am honored to be a part of one such as this."

Cole only hoped Rylie thought so as well. She seemed

to be taking a long time, and he reached out to Ryan. She said they were pulling into the drive now and would be out in a few minutes. Almost as soon as Cole heard the doors slamming at the front of the house, William tensed up.

"I can hear her." Cole told him what Ryan had told him. "She is excited to meet me but has already decided I'm too good for her. Why would a woman feel that way about someone they've never met?"

"Why did you lurk around corners watching her when you could have easily met her?" Cole laughed at the expression on William's face when Dillon spoke. "She's going to be all right. I have no idea why I feel that way, but I do the more I speak with you. However, remember what I told you. You hurt her, and your life will not be worth the bullet it takes to kill you."

As soon as Rylie came out onto the deck, she walked to William and slapped him hard. Cole stood up when the man shifted. His body was so much taller than his mate that it would take very little for him to hurt her. But all he did was lay on the deck before her, his belly there for her to rip open should she want.

"The next time you have something to say to me, you come to me. Understand?" The were whimpered, then nodded. "Why am I having to find out about you from every one of my family members when I've seen you twice now? Damn it, I won't start this out on a bad note. Come with me."

As she moved off in the direction William had come from, William looked up at Cole.

"You'd better get moving, William. If she gets to wherever she's going, and you're not there, there will be hell to pay." The beast got up and started after his mate. Before he got to her, Cole and the rest of them could hear her yelling at him. "I think she has this under control, don't you guys?"

They were still laughing as the couple disappeared into the woods. Whatever was on the other side was going to be the perfect place for the two of them to get to know each other. The others left, laughing and hugging each other as they got into their cars.

When Ryan turned to him, he laughed when she said to come with her. Cole followed her up the stairs like a good dragon. He knew what was in store for him, and he would have followed her to the moon and back. Cole had never been so happy as he was at that very moment.

Closing the door behind him when he entered their bedroom, he stood there leaning against it as Ryan stood by the bed. She didn't speak as she began taking her clothing off. He didn't either when he decided to help her. By the time he got to her skin, he was hard as a rock and willing to bet that he wasn't going to last all that long as soon as he touched her. Cole didn't care. They had the rest of their lives to make love. Pulling her into his arms, Cole kissed her.

Chapter 6

The kiss was much more than she had ever expected from a man. It wasn't just sexy, but it was claiming, calming too. When he lifted his mouth from hers, she looked into his eyes and saw his dragon. He was so beautiful that she put her hands on Cole's cheeks so that she could watch him there.

"He loves you." Ryan said she loved him as well. That he was a part of him that she would forever love. "I'm glad to hear that. I love you as well, Ryan. With all that I am. All that I will ever be, I will love you until I am no more."

He kissed her again, running his hands slowly down her body. When he cupped her ass in his hands, she felt herself being lifted up and his cock right at her entrance. Before she could wonder what he was going to do next, Cole sat her on the edge of the bed and stepped back from it.

"I've thought of nothing else but tasting you. Feasting on your body so I can know your scent, your taste." He got down on his knees and put her legs on either side of his shoulders. The coolness of his breath made her wet, and she tried to put her legs back together, embarrassed. "Don't, love. I can smell you. You smell delicious."

The first touch of his tongue to her wet clit had her coming up off the bed in a climax that took her breath away. Even before she could regain some of her composure, he was doing just as he said he would. Cole was feasting on her pussy.

Ryan came so many times she was weak with it. Every time she thought he would be finished, his big body shifting around, she'd come again with just a touch. It didn't matter if it was his tongue or his fingers, all he had to do was touch her needy flesh, and she'd be screaming out his name again and again.

Finally, when he stood up, she was ready to tell him she'd had enough. That there wasn't any way, she could come once more. Then she got a long look at the man in front of her. Sitting up just enough that she could look fully at Cole, her body tightened in anticipation for whatever he wanted to do to her.

His skin was dewy with sweat from what he'd been doing to her. There wasn't much in the way of hair on his chest, but he did have a line of it that went to his cock. Following the line down, Ryan sat up and touched her fingers to the tip of his dark full cock. His moan had her wrapping her hand around him. Her fingers wouldn't touch; he was so thick.

"You keep that up and I'm never going to get to be inside of you when I come. And that is something I've needed for a very long time." She moved back, sitting up enough to watch him as he moved closer to her. Telling her to scoot up on the bed, she watched his face as she did what she was told. When he was over her, he smiled. "I don't know how long I'm going to last, love. The thought of coming deep inside of you is making me mad with the need to come now."

He filled her. There were no words to describe how it felt to have him there. They were one. They were mates. And when he moved, his cock filling her over and over, Ryan had to hold onto him, or she knew she'd simply break apart, fly away and never be able to tell him how very much she loved him.

Watching his face was beautiful. Even when he was strained, his body tense, he looked deeply into her eyes. When he pulled her to him, lifting her ass up tighter to his body, Ryan let her body go and came hard enough that she didn't have breath in her body. The scream lodged in her throat seemed to be a testament to how amazing it felt. Blacking out, she didn't have a single thought in her head but love. Loving this man was all she had ever needed or would ever want again.

When she opened her eyes, she could see that Cole

was close. Moving her hips just a little, giving him more of herself, his body bowed back, and she saw his dragon race over his skin like he too was coming with his host. Then she felt his release.

The heat of him filled her from top to bottom. She held tighter onto his shoulders, digging deeply into his skin, so she broke the skin. Feeling blood beneath her nails, she moved to let it fall into her mouth.

As soon as his blood touched her tongue, she knew she'd just found paradise. A utopia that was so beautiful, so amazing that she had to close her eyes when it became too much. Coming then, her body high on his blood, Ryan felt her world darken around her until there was nothing left.

Waking up, she reached for Cole. If he was there, he was just out of her reach. Sitting up in the bed, she found him by the window. He was sitting in the wingback chair by the fireplace in their room. Saying his name had him turning to look at her. She was ever so glad to see him smiling.

"I thought for sure that I broke you." She said she had thought so as well. "Christ, that was nothing like I've ever experienced before. And I'm really old."

"Thank you for not pointing out how much practice you have had." She sat up, pulling the blanket around her as she did so. "Why are you up? Did something happen?"

"No. Nothing at all. You were sleeping so well that

I didn't want to bother you. And it's just after midnight, so I was waiting for the night creatures to come out." Cole patted his lap, and she went to sit on him. "If you look over by the pool, you can see movement. Once they figure out that they're being watched, they'll signal to the others that there are other creatures about."

Ryan watched as the ground suddenly became bright with blinking lights. She was sure there were thousands of them. She told Cole she'd thought those were fireflies.

"They are, in a way. The ones that children catch are decoys so the others can complete their work. They do their best work at night, I'm told. They'll go along the yard, being ever so quiet, and pick up seeds that have fallen from trees. Or from flowers that have gone to seed. When they have their packs full, they'll race to the bag nearby to fill it. Someone, one of the elders, will watch over the bag so that no human finds it. After they've finished their work, the bag and all the little fae will go to another part of the forest to gather what they can there." She asked him why they didn't just let them sprout where they had fallen. "It's a long process of finding seeds to replant. Their diligence is what makes the earth regenerate after a fire or flood. They have the seeds from the area affected, and replant them so others might be able to feed from them."

"What a wonderful tale." She watched as the lights began to move toward the tree line. When they stopped moving, she was afraid for them. "What is it? Do they need someone out there to protect them?"

"They do. Watch. I told you that William was part fae. It's him that is the spot in the middle of them. I think he is with your sister." She watched as the shapes became clearer when the fae lit up the area. It was her sister. Rylie was standing next to William. "I'm sure he's introducing them to her. They'll think of her as one of them before the night is over. I'm not really sure of a lot of fae traditions, but I'd be willing to bet that Rylie will have magic beyond what she had before."

They sat there for another hour, watching the fae circle around the couple in the middle of them. The bright lights, she noticed, weren't just white, but all the colors. She wished she could ask her sister what was going on, but a part of her thought that Rylie would be embarrassed to know they were being spied upon. When they all moved into the forest and out of sight, she turned and looked at Cole.

"Now what?" After he laughed, a burst of humor that she was sure caught him off guard, she smiled at him. "That didn't come out right. What I meant to ask you is what do we do now that we're a couple. I'm sure things have changed. I don't want to be caught unaware of shit that might happen."

"I haven't any idea. As I've been told by all the other dragons, the wives have gotten different types of magic that even their mates don't have. I believe in this case; we'll have to wing it." She said she wasn't good at winging things. "Yes, I know that about you. You like things in neat order. But there is little that we can do about it at this point. Other than just watch the others and see if you can do what they can. I got some extra magic too. As I said before, I haven't any idea what it— Holy shit, I forgot."

He stood her on the floor and went to his dresser. She knew he wasn't getting clothing because they could both dress themselves. Cole came back with an envelope in his hand and pulled her back onto his lap. Handing it to her, she asked him what it was.

"The attorney for the insurance company came by this morning—well, I guess yesterday morning—while you were out with Dillon finding him furniture. He said that your brother and sister were getting an envelope as well. I asked him what it was about, and he said there was an accompanying letter that would make it understood." Ryan wondered if it was money. "I don't know, and neither will you until you open it up."

Tearing into the envelope, she nearly dropped the check that was in it, wrapped inside the letter. Cole held the check while she read what was said. Ryan read the highlights to Cole.

"It says that the insurance policies taken out on my parents were good policies. And as we had nothing to do with the death of our parents, the insurance company decided, since we saved them so much heartache and bad publicity, they'd honor it by paying us for finding out what Sandra had been up to." She looked at Cole when he whistled. "What is it? And I can't think that we should get any of this money. It was Dillon's name on the policy."

"I think you should look at the amount, babe." She did then read off the number aloud. It didn't make it seem any less real. "They gave each of you two million dollars in the form of a cashier's check. You could give it to your brother if that's what you want. To us, financially, it won't make a lot of difference if we have this or not. And since I know that William has a great deal of money too, I'm assuming it won't matter to him either."

"A lot of people would be thrilled to have this kind of money. I mean, even as recent as a few weeks ago, I would have been happy to have it. I'm not saying we couldn't find some use for it, but I'm thinking Dillon can make it into more. For himself." Cole asked her if he'd see it that way. "No. But I can make him see it my way."

They were still talking about the check when they made their way down to the kitchen. She'd completely forgotten that their cook was a faerie. When she went from the tiny creature sitting on the table to the very unhuman looking person in front of the stove, it sent Ryan into a fit of giggles that she couldn't stop.

"You have sparkles all over you." Bertha laughed along with her. When she showed her her ears, they both got to laughing hard while Cole just stared at the two of them. "We have a sparkly cook. I have no idea why I find that so funny. I'm sorry."

"Don't be. I'm happy you're having fun. I could be big all the time, but I do enjoy being a little person that can fly around should I want to." Ryan asked her if she didn't want to be their cook. "Oh, yes, I do. To be able to be with you and your dragon is quite a thing for faeries. To be able to say that I work for the lord of the castle, and him being a dragon is just icing on the cookies. I get so many perks from the other faeries too. Nothing I don't share, but it's fun to know that some are a wee bit jealous."

"Do faeries need things like we would? What I mean is, do faeries have doctors and places for the elderly to live? I'm not being rude here, but I know so very little about your kind. If I've offended you, I'm sorry." Bertha said she hadn't and that she loved the questions. "I have come into some money, and I was thinking I'd like to help your kind. You and the others, you've done so much for me that I would love to be able to do something for you."

"There is always a need for more shelters for us. But as you can imagine, there isn't much need for a large house or building. Flowers would be great. However, the others, they make sure they plant more than they'll need so we might have what we've a need for."

Bertha sat a large platter of food in front of them. Ryan was thinking they were going to share the food, but she also set one down in front of Cole. He dug into his like he'd been starved. She supposed he might be. They had burnt a great many calories.

"Let me think on this, my lady. I can get with the others and figure out what we can use. It won't need to be big, just so you know. We've been making what we need for a very long time."

"I'm betting you could use more materials." Bertha put a glass of juice in front of her and told her that she'd need to drink more fluids as she went about making a list of things when she thought of them. She did ask her what sort of materials she was thinking. "Well, cloth for one thing. I know you can basically wear what you want, right?"

"Nay, we have to get ourselves dressed. But that is a good point. Material for new clothing would be good. And small buttons. I so love buttons." She showed her the shoes she had on. "When I find some that I can affix to my clothing, I put it there. I think them a good invention."

Ryan wondered what she'd think of Velcro but didn't bring it up. She did, however, start on her own list. Surely she could find something she could get for them to use to make their lives better. She'd not need the amount of the check, she knew, so the original plan, to give it to her brother, would still work. Ryan knew that Dillon would make it count for something good too.

After eating nearly all the food on her plate, she made her way to the office she'd claimed yesterday. There were several messages on her desk, but she pushed them aside, for now, to check on her emails. There were three from her former boss, as well as two from the bank in town. She looked them over first.

She needed to go to the bank to sign some paperwork. That was good because she needed to get some things squared away in town anyway. When Cole knocked at her door, she looked up at him and smiled.

"I have to run a few things by Devon's place. I was wondering if you wanted to go and hang out with Kelly." Ryan told him she would love that but was way behind on things here. "I thought you'd say that. I can get there and plead with Devon that I have to go home, so he doesn't keep me all day. Not that I mind spending time with him, but I have been putting things off for some time now."

Getting her head buried back into what she'd been working on, Ryan never got around to opening the emails from the president. The man was literally driving her crazy. She didn't want the job of running the FBI. That would mean she'd have to move back to her home and not be here all the time. She loved this new town and the people that lived here.

It was nearing dinner time when her phone rang. It was Stanley again.

"I'm not going to ask you to head up the department. I just need to ask you a few questions about something else. As much as I would love to try and talk you into it, I've heard from one of your sisters-in-law, and they made it clear that you're not going to be moving back here anytime soon." She asked him which sister she had to thank for that. "All of them. But I do need your input on a couple of things. It can be done on the phone too. There are fourteen files on the desk of your former boss. I can't make heads nor tails out of what the hell they're about. Some of them have really old dates on them, while a few of them have only just been opened. What do you know about fae? I know that's a really strange question, but he swore that there were little pixies around that did magic for, of all things, dragons."

Ryan didn't so much as blink at her end of the call. "What do you mean, pixies? And did he think there were dragons too?" He read to her one of the things that Arnold Baskin had written on sticky notes in one of the files. "So he figured out that there are really faeries, and that brought him to the conclusion that there were dragons. What do you want me to do about this? I mean, what did you think I could answer for you?"

"I don't know. But there is a note here that he was going to meet with a person that claimed they knew where the dragons were living. It has an address here that is just on a residential street. Why would he think a dragon could be able to live in a home?" He sighed heavily. "I guess what I'm asking you about is this—in your years of working with him, did Arnold ever give you the indication that he was a little touched in the head?"

"No. Not once. He didn't care for me working for

him as a woman unless you count what kind of jobs he wanted me to do for him. Other than that, he seemed all right, I guess. This address you have, have you checked it out?" He told her it was a house, and he didn't need to check it out. "I have this map thing that I can pull up for anywhere in the world. Can I have the address, please? I'd like to see if this place is a monstrous home or something. I mean, that might be all that had him thinking about dragons. Perhaps he thought a big house must be dragons."

"Christ, I hope not." He gave her the address, and she plugged it into the map search. "What you see there is a home with a swing set in the back yard, as well as a pool house. I would think he'd at least have looked for larger homes with trees all around. I don't know why I called you, now that I think about it. I just really wanted you to tell me that he had been off his rocker and should have been retired years ago."

Hanging up with the president, she sat there for a long time. She had to tell someone, but who did she go to with this? If it was a real dragon, he would have to be warned. Picking up the phone, she called the only person she knew who could get this done.

"Hello, Devon."

~*~

Devon put the phone back in the cradle and sat there for several minutes. Rocking his daughter was a great deal of fun, but he knew he'd have to put her down to conduct the business at hand. He hated that more than anything. Having time with his daughter was the highlight of his afternoon.

After putting her into her playpen, he picked up the roster that had all the names of the dragons in it. There were addresses too, but a great many of them hadn't been updated for fifty or so years. Finding the address was easy enough. A dragon did live there too.

How did he go about telling the dragon that was supposed to have lived there that he'd been found? Thinking about it had him making notes on the subject, only to cross them out and put down something else. It was a delicate operation, finding out who lived in the house. He reached out for Nicole, the protector of them all, and asked her to come by his office. Please.

I'm sort of in the middle of something right now. Is it important? He told her just what Ryan had told him. *I'll be right there. Don't laugh at what I'm wearing either. Or so help me, I'll make you regret it.*

As soon as she popped into his office, he had to cover his mouth. The glare that she gave him had him hoping he could keep from getting himself hurt. But he did find himself curious as to why she'd be dressed as a clown in the middle of the day. Finally, it was just too much for him, and he had to ask.

"Remember about six months ago? We hired this guy to go around to the schools to give away toothbrushes and paste to all the kids?" Devon said he didn't know they'd been dressing up. "I didn't either when I told him I'd cover for him today. All he told me was that my uniform would be brought over to me. By the way, we're going to get him a better costume. The one he brought me smelled like old shoes that had been in a locker for six months. Also, while I think candy with a toothbrush would be an oxymoron, I think we should give them something besides this little bag of shit."

"I like the one you have on. I'm assuming you made it?" She said she'd rather not have to wear the one he'd brought her. "I don't blame you. I'll get on finding something to go with the baggies. But this thing with the Feds, we need to figure out what else this agent knew, as well as where he might well have gotten his information. Even if there isn't a dragon there, he was looking."

"I've sent one of the ghosts that work with Roxanna to see what they can figure out with the files. This may be just a one time thing, and we'll not have to worry overly much, but I'm not willing to take that chance."

He said that he was not either.

When Newt showed up in the room with him, Devon knew they had more than just a little problem.

"They got themselves a whole fistful of them suckers. I'm just getting to be able to read, but they was marked important. I got me a looksee into one of them, and there is also mention of witches thereabout." Devon asked the kid would he be able to bring the files to him. "Not unless you are a wanting me to get my butt kicked around. I'm not to take stuff from those kinds of buildings. They got themselves a lot of cameras and such. While they can't see me, they can see the stuff I'm moving around. Makes it harder on the ones that live there to be doing that to them. Bringing attention, I mean."

"There are ghosts living in the Fed building?" Newt grinned at him and told him what they were. "Oh. Followers. I guess they're hanging around with the ones they knew before. All right. We'll have to do something about this. If for no other reason than to warn the others that they're being watched."

It took them three hours to get a plan worked out. It might well have been quicker if Newt hadn't kept waking up his daughter and wanting to play with her. Even Nicole, dressed now in jeans, was having fun playing with the child. Finally, they sent one of the faeries to the house to have a look around.

When Bubble returned, she didn't look happy. Asking her if she'd been harmed by the others, she said that their living conditions were poor and that they were unemployed as well. Devon asked her what he could do for them.

"They need a home that can accommodate them, your lordship. Right now, there are five adult dragons living in the little house, with no way of making sure they have a place to be themselves. Dragons need a place that they can be quiet in. Also, I found this to be fretful; there is not one faerie there to help them with their needs. I think them to be hurting for that as well." He asked her if there were faeries that could be sent to them. "Yes. I can line up several now that can go and spread some magic around the house so they'll have more room. I do believe them to need jobs also. There is very little work there for them."

After she was able to send out some emergency help, he called on Dillon to come and see what sort of dragon owned businesses were in the area. Having the younger man around had been extremely helpful in the last few days. Not only had he been helping with investments, but he was making up a chart for them to use when they were asking questions about companies that wanted to come to the area.

In less than another hour, they had faeries at the home as well as enough magic to keep them all safe. They were being fed now, which hadn't been something the other dragons had a great deal of money for. Also, and this pleased him a great deal, Dillon was able to not only set them up jobs, but he also made sure they had transportation. Now they only had to see what other names were on files at the Fed building.

Devon was still at his desk when they got word from the offices. Not only did they have about fifty addresses for dragons and other creatures, but the agents also had a list of people they thought would help them identify shifters. While a great many people knew what they were, there were people still out there looking for a way to capture a shifter for the money they'd bring on the open market. Devon wanted to save them all.

"I've made a few dozen phone calls on your behalf." He thanked Ryan for her help. "Don't thank me just yet. There are several issues that only you can take care of. Or ordain me or something so that when I speak for you, they know it. The fuckers said that since I'm with the king ding dong, then I should know the rules."

"They didn't actually call me king ding dong, did they?" Ryan only shrugged. "I think you're a bigger pain in the ass than any two of the others living around here. Also, I don't ordain you. That's a religious thing. But I can make it so that they know your word is the same as mine. So long as you clear up the fact that I'm not a ding dong."

"You know what you are? A fun sucker." Devon laughed with her. "There are two dragons that need their asses kicked too. Once I started speaking to them, they started making noises about how you owe them. I never quite got what you owed them or why, but they're pissy about it. I'm going to take Kelly with me the next time I go there. Oh, they have a meeting hall that they use. It's covered in magic, so they only look like some kind of idiot's club for men. They don't allow the womenfolk— their words, not mine—to know about things that go on in the meeting."

"It used to be that way until someone figured out that the females knew more about survival than the males did. After that, they conducted the meetings and also made sure that people were taken care of. These dragons, where did you find them?" She told him. "Not that far. You'd think I'd have more to do with them than just figuring out they're unsatisfied with my work. I think you're right about giving you the power you need to make them know that what you're saying is from me."

"I was joking." He nodded. "You've already done it, haven't you? Given me some shit that is going to make me pissed off."

"Everything I do pisses you off. But yes, I've done it. Also, I would like for you to take Kelly with you. Also, Jackson or Nicole. If that doesn't work, then I'm going to go with you. They're not going to be happy if that happens."

When she left him, he went about setting up meetings all around the world that he could send Ryan to. She wasn't diplomatic, but she did make people understand their situation. Bubble had told him a little about the meeting she'd had, and he knew she was the right person for the job. He only hoped she didn't have to use the power she now had. She could kill a dragon with just a snap of her fingers.

Chapter 7

"I think I have a way for you to get the book of all dragons updated, as well as getting with all the dragons on that list." Cole got a much-needed kiss from Ryan as he sat down in Devon's office. "It's not my idea entirely, but the faeries that have been helping me gather things up. Basically, we call to all the faeries that have died that had the care of a dragon. All dragons."

"Will calling them work?" Cole told Devon he was having Jackson and Nicole work on it right now. "That might well be a lot of faeries. Don't you think?"

"Yes. But with the magic of bringing them to the book, they've already worked out with Bryce and Noah that all the faerie has to do to give the information to the book is to touch it. It will automatically fill out whatever they have in their mind. That part works. Bryce said that if we can get the other part to work, the knowledge to be brought to us by the dead, she's going to use it for her books as well. I think this is going to be a great tool for now and in the future." Cole looked over at Ryan and could tell she'd been crying. "What's wrong, honey? Did Devon say something to you?"

"No. I mean, yes, he did, but it's fine now. It wasn't mean, you know like he usually can be." Devon said she wasn't nice. "I just found out some of the things Sandra did to some friends of mine while she was still married to Dillon. I'm just thankful he was able to survive her. She wasn't ever a nice person."

"That's an understatement. Ryan was also talking to me about her windfall. She and her brother and sister are going to pool the money and put it towards something for the community. We were going over a few things I have here that they can work on as a team." As Devon spoke, Ryan handed Cole a couple of the sheets he'd not noticed on her lap. "Those are the ones she wants to present to the other two. They're going to do this smartly and only put in one-third of what they have, and invest the rest so it can keep up with whatever projects they decide on."

Cole looked at Devon when Ryan got up to leave. She said she'd be back, but he could tell she was crying again. Devon waited for the door to his office to close before he spoke to him. It was in low tones, so he doubted that Ryan would hear.

"She just found out that Sandra had taken out life

insurance policies on Dillon, as well as her and Rylie. They had the same rider on them that said there would be twice the amount if they were killed in an accident." Cole asked him why he'd not waited on him to tell her that. "I didn't tell her. She found out from the insurance company this morning when they called. I guess that is why they didn't mind paying the three of them the money. With them living, the company didn't have to pay out money for the deaths of such nice people. It's hurt her to know that they meant so little to Sandra."

"I can see that." Devon asked him about the magic. After telling him everything they were doing with it, Ryan came back to join them. She'd been crying again, but knowing what it was about, while it didn't appease him much, he did understand it better. "I have a job for you should you want to take it on. It's not that big of a deal, but I have to get it done. It's only four months until the holidays, and we need to start heading up some of the charities we usually do for the community. Actually, we should have already started on them, but with the way things have been going, I got a little behind."

"What he's not telling you is that he forgot about it. Since he's been all wrapped up with having a baby around, the rest of the world has ceased to exist." Devon didn't even deny what Cole said. He grinned like a loon, then asked if they wanted to see some pictures. The baby was sleeping next to the desk as it was now. Pictures were necessary. "Well, I have three things I have to get done before noon. So, if you want to meet me for lunch in town, Ryan, I'd love it. Unless you're too busy."

"I'm never too busy for the love of my life. You let me know when you're ready, and I'll be there for you." She kissed him on the mouth and nearly skipped out of the room.

Cole looked at Devon. "What were the two plans? If you don't mind telling me. I didn't even look at what she handed me. I was so concerned with her crying."

"One of them is a gathering place for senior citizens. It won't be a nursing home, but a place that all seniors can visit and be around people their own age. However, she is talking with some of the pack and other shifters to see if they'll have some of the older people in their groups come out and work with them on crafts and the like. She seems to think that since the pack takes such good care of their elderly, they'll enjoy having a little bit of time to get busy." Cole said he liked that idea. "I do, as well. I told her that if she and the others didn't pick that one, I'd do it. The other job is a good one too. I think that in order to get them both taken care of, even though she really is leaning toward this one, she'll convince the other two that they can get two for the price of one. It's to do with putting in a large pool and snack house for the community. Remember the one we had here about fifty years ago? It finally had to be filled in when it got to the point no one wanted to go there anymore. It was a done deal before I found out, or I might well have already put in a pool for the town."

They talked for another hour. Cole did get around to asking him if he'd spoken to William or Rylie, and he told him the only person to have spoken to either of them was Ryan. She seemed pleased that they were so happy.

"Ryan is going to try matchmaking with her brother next." They both groaned. "I agree with you on that. But it's not setting him up on blind dates. It's getting him out of the house and office so he can see others. She's afraid he'll close himself off from the world and not be a part of it. I guess he's done this before. He is afraid of getting hurt again."

"Him being married to Sandra must have been difficult on them all. I did remember to tell him about the magic she had. But I guess he'd already figured that out." Devon looked at the door, then back at him. "I still see her in the courtroom. The way she just started to dry up. I think the worst part was when she reached out to Bryce there at the end, her fingers pointing then just falling off. Christ, I hope never to see something like that ever again. Every time I see a pile of ash, I will think of that woman."

Jackson came into the room in his usual way, banging the door open so it hit the wall on the other side and speaking like they were already part of the conversation when he started it. It took them both three tries to get him to slow down and bring them up to date on what he'd been talking about when entering the room.

"Christ, I wish you two would pay attention. We got

it to work." Devon looked at him again, and Cole could see the confusion on his face. The same look, he'd bet, that was on his own face. "The magic to bring the faeries to us. We—well, mostly Nicole—got it to work. She is not only able to bring forth the watchers of the dead, but also a way for them to tell her where the dragons are so their resting places can be taken care of by the living."

"Is that in the book?" Jackson said it wasn't, but there was a section for notes. "So that's what you put in there. Brilliant. And like you said, once we know where the dead are, we can make sure they're taken care of, much like they did for the world when they were living."

By the time they had worked out all the details for the book, Cole was ready to call it a day. He loved all his friends, would do anything for them. But spending a lot of time with them in one sitting was hard on a body. Sometimes it was the laughing so hard that he hurt or anger at something that had happened. It was exhausting, but he didn't think he could live without them around. Getting up, he told Devon he'd do the project that he needed.

Cole was sitting at his desk, going over the things that were needed for the upcoming holidays, when he felt someone in the room with him. When he looked around, there wasn't anyone that he could see immediately and decided that since he was a big assed dragon, he could command the person to show themselves. If he didn't like them, he'd just have to—

"You're strange." The pixie was sitting on his blotter, looking up at him. "I have come to see you about a few matters pertaining to the dead that are being called forth."

"I'm not the one in charge of that. I'm not saying I can't answer your concerns, but I want you to know it's for the betterment of the dragons left behind." She said it wasn't about that. "Then what's on your mind? And what is your name, please?"

"Rankheart. Will there be recrimination to the ones that come to you?" Cole asked her what she meant. "Some of them need to know that they didn't fail the dragons they were watching over. A great many of them, living and dead, are shameful of the fact that their charges were killed or murdered. They're in hiding now, and when they are called, they might end their lives rather than face the consequences. What will happen to those that feel as if they did wrong by allowing their dragon to die?"

"No one needs to feel that they failed anyone." She just stared at him. "I'm serious. There were times when, if not for my faerie when I was at war or even going about my daily chores, I might well have foolhardily harmed both of us. It wouldn't have been her responsibility if I had gone ahead and acted without her input."

"The faeries, they are thinking that once they are brought before the king to lay their information on the book, they will be destroyed." Cole told Rankheart that would never happen. "You are sure of that? The king of dragons, he is said to be a monster. That he killed our kind by making them suffer in ways that no one will be able to witness with a strong gut."

"Have you met the new king?" She tilted her head and looked at him. "You are aware that there is a new king of dragons, aren't you? Not only is there Devon and his queen Kelly, but he also has a mated couple that have been proclaimed as the protector of all dragons. That would include any that served with them in life or death."

"I have been in hiding." He told her he was sorry. "You say this is a new king. How do you know he is as kind as you say? For all you know, he could be just as much a monster as the one before him."

"Would you like to meet him?" She said yes. He could tell she really did want to believe him as well. Reaching out to Devon, he told him what was going on and where he was. Devon said he was out and about and would come there first thing. "He's on his way here, Rankheart. Once he gets here, I assure you that you're going to see a man who is not just truthful in his word and bond, but a man that will go out of his way in order to make life much easier for those like you. I'm terribly sorry you didn't know he was around."

He had Bertha bring him some scones and flowers for their guest. When Ryan showed up a few minutes later, she introduced herself to the pixie and told her what she'd been doing. The pool was a big hit with Rankheart in that the faeries could use some of the water for their own if need be.

"It will have chemicals in it. But you just gave me a good idea. How would you like it if I were to make it so that you and the others had an endless supply of water that was clean and pure?" Rankheart asked Ryan if she was real. "Real? I suppose I am. But other than that, I don't know what you mean."

"No one just makes things for faeries. Not that many people believe in us anymore." Ryan told her that she did, and she would do just what she told her she would. "Well, I guess we'll see. As I said, no one does things they say they will for us little creatures."

Cole wanted to warn the little woman but thought she might learn that being a flippant ass when someone was trying to help you was in bad form. He sat back in his chair as Ryan geared up her loins and let her temper fly on the little woman.

"You little piece of shit. Who shit in your fucking oats today? And where do you get off judging me when we've only just met? I'm not used to people calling me a liar, but to do so to my face is just beyond rude. Christ. You need to get that stick out of your ass and start bending a little until you see the lay of the ground." Ryan stood up then and looked down on Rankheart. "Watch your words wisely, little one. I'm much more powerful than you'll ever be on your good days. Should you have any."

Devon walked in as Rankheart was being dressed down. He had his daughter with him, which he supposed was to make him less intimidating. It would have worked except for the look on his face. Not only was he as angry as Cole had ever seen him, but he was also letting enough of his dragon go that there was no mistaking his wrath.

"You will cease this immediately." Cole stood up. He wouldn't allow him to speak to his mate that way. But before he could defend her, Devon handed him the baby and stood near Ryan and looked at Rankheart. "You will not talk to my family like this. I know your family, Rankheart the Red. I know they have colored your outlook on life in general. But this isn't your family, they're mine, and you will not treat them like they have done nothing but lie and cheat you their entire life."

Rankheart laid down on the desk where she'd been standing up to Ryan. As soon as she did that, he could see the anger wash off Devon like he'd been standing in a storm, and it cleansed him. Rankheart the Red was giving her life over to Devon for what she'd done.

~*~

Noah listened to the information being told to him. It was a great deal too. When Rankheart was finished, he looked down at his notes. Thankfully, he'd had a pen in his hand when she started, or he might well have missed a lot of it. He had also been able to star the things she told him so that he could get more information on it.

"First of all, this is awesome. I don't think we would have known all this without your help." Devon had told him that Rankheart didn't get much in the way of positive feedback. So if she deserved it, he said to tell her. "There are a couple of points I'd like to clear up with you. I don't understand some of the language you're using."

"It's pixie." He told her he thought that faeries were all pixies. "No. We're a different kind altogether. Not in great numbers like the faeries are, but we are around to work with the others. One of the big differences is that we can be bigger should we want to and not have to stay that way. Bertha is one of us. She's been around for a long time too. Though I think she says she's faerie so as not to confuse people. What is it you don't understand?"

He showed her on his notes the part where she said that they were *gully gipped*. Not only did she explain that it meant the pixies in question were overweight from a lack of jobs, but she was able to change herself into one, so he'd understand it better.

"I'm assuming this is a bad thing." Rankheart told him that those types of pixies were too fat to even get up to toddle off to their bed when 'twas time. "Lazy then. That's what we call lazy humans. Okay. One more here that I have is *wanker doodle*. I have an idea what wanker means in human language, but not with you."

"I'm sure it's the same. It's a male pixie that thinks his wanker, his manly parts, should be used on every female that will allow him to. My brother, he was one such as that. He's no longer with us, as he tried to wanker his way into the bed of another pixie. She'd been willing, but her mate, he wasn't so keen on the idea." Noah covered his laughter with a short cough. "Also, I didn't mention it to you, but when you hear that someone is being called a bug dweller, it is a dead pixie."

"Yes, well, that one is very clear, isn't it?" He was having such a wonderful time with the little pixie that he forgot they were working. "Is there anything else I should know before we have Devon start calling in his pixies?"

"Why does he want to do this?" Noah asked her what she meant. "Bring them in. Have them put their information in the big book. There is no reason for it. I mean, they're dead, aren't they? They did a great service for sure. No one else cared enough to make sure they knew where they were."

"But we do now." She just shook her head. "Okay, maybe you need to know a little bit about us, the dragons that are here working every day in not only making it easier for pixies but all living creatures. That would include humans too. When I first met Devon and the others, I was nothing more than a man trying my best to make it in the world. I was a human that happened to be friends with the strongest dragon there was. He called me one day, even going to far as to sending his wife out to get me just so I could help with the things he had going."

"You're not human." He told her he wasn't anymore. He was a dragon. "I don't understand. They cannot do that. Change someone into what they aren't."

"Yes, you're absolutely right on that. But I wasn't changed, Rankheart. I was given a great gift. A gift of a dragon that put itself inside of me to have me be just like the others. A magic so strong it even surprised those that were here when it happened. Kelly, the mate to Devon, she too was given the gift of being a dragon. Her dragon was at one time the dragon for Devon's mother." She asked him if he was sure that was how it had happened. "Absolutely sure."

She started pacing back and forth before she spoke again. When he asked her if she needed him to answer any more questions, she asked him if she could be bigger. Not exactly sure what that might mean to her, he nodded before he could think how big she was going to be.

However, she turned into a lovely female. The glitter was still there, her wings too. It was harder to figure out the finer details on her when she'd been small, but he could see now that she was something of an oddity to the other pixies that had been coming around. She was wearing a crown, and she had a long blade at her back. Even it was encrusted with gems and the like that sparkled around the room like a disco ball might have.

When she paced, this time on the floor, he could see little parts of her sparkle fall upon the floor. It made him smile when he thought about how much she was like her king. A pacer, as well as one that thought hard before saying anything that might well come back and bite him in the ass. It was why people and creatures alike underestimated Devon. He wasn't being laid back when he spoke to you but looking for the place to stick the knife if he had to murder you.

"There are more." Noah had a feeling that while he was musing, he might well have missed something she'd told him. "Other wisps. Other, like you said you got, other dragons' spirits that were released when their holder was killed."

"Do you mean it's common to have a dragon release his other self in order to save the wisps for other dragons to be made?" Rankheart nodded. "Are there a great many of them? I mean, they're very small, as you are most of the time. They're just the spirits of the dragons that become one when they find hosts, correct? How many do you—?" He let out a breath. "I'm calmer now. How many other wisps, like you called them, are out there?"

"Hundreds." He asked her to repeat what she'd said. "It's going to take us a long day and more if I have to keep repeating things you don't believe. I was gonna say thousands, but you tend to get all wonky eyed when I say stuff like that. But there are thousands of them, just waiting for someone to come along and meet them. If they like the person within, the wisps can enter their body, much like they did with Lady Kelly, and make them a dragon too. They've been with me. I've been keeping them safe."

With trembling hands, Noah picked up his phone. Setting it back down on its cradle, he had to count to ten three times before he thought he could speak like a man and not squeak like a little mouse. When he thought he could call Devon, he picked up the phone and completely forgot how to use the number pad. He looked at Dillon when he entered the room with them.

"I need help." Dillon told him he looked as if he did. "Would you mind calling Noah— No, that's me. Don't call me. Call Devon for me. Yes, that's him." Noah knocked over his pencil container and began gathering them up. "I don't even know why I got these things. They're very un-useful if you ask me. Why, just the other day, I picked one of them up to use, and the point broke off. There are thousands of them, you know." Dillon told him he'd buy him more. "No. Not pencils, but wisps."

Devon must have answered. "Can you come over here, please? I think Noah has lost his mind." The pause had Noah thinking he should be offended at Dillon's words, but he was still working out the thousands of wisps. "You might want to bring over some pencils if you have them. For some reason, he's obsessed with wanting a lot of those."

"It's not...never mind. Dillon, this is Rankheart. Rankheart, this is Dillon. Another family member." They stared at each other. That was when he noticed there was a glow around Rankheart that he'd not noticed before. "Is that why they call you the Red? That you glow red all the time?"

"Nay, 'tis not. The red is for blood. I was—I am a

warrior that strikes fear into the hearts of those I come up against." She looked around the room, then back at Dillon. "You're not what I thought you'd be. You're not human either. What are you, if you don't mind me asking?"

"No. Christ, you're beautiful. I guess you'd know that." She didn't nod, nor did she disagree with Dillon. "Does this mean what I think it does? I mean, my sisters, they both told me that it hit you right in the heart and in the head."

"What hit you?" Noah did get offended when they both told him to shut up at the same time. "I'm only trying to ascertain what you're talking about. I might well have something to add to the conversation. Why is everyone so blasted mean today?"

"He's my mate." Noah said that couldn't be it. That he had a mate. "Not you, you dunderhead. The man here. Mr. Dillon. Him being my mate changes things now. Don't you see that?"

Noah was still working around the thousand when he realized he was alone in the room except for Devon. And he'd been there for some time if the lack of scones on the little plate was any indication, as well as the half empty glass of tea. Even the sweat around the outside of the glass seemed to be mocking him for his lack of paying attention. Noah looked at his friend when he laughed.

"You've been mumbling to yourself for some time now, my friend." He told him what he'd been working out. "Yes, I've been made aware of that too, while you were fussing with your desk toys. Why do you even have those bouncing balls on your desk? They're too small to throw at anyone with any kind of accuracy." He showed him how they worked. "Oh well, that's not any clearer."

Noah decided right then and there that he'd had enough of people taking potshots at him today. Standing up, he went to find his lovely mate. Surely Bryce would have something nice to say to him. But as soon as he walked into the kitchen where she was, he turned and left. He was not going to get in on a conversation about Christmas when it was barely past the Fourth of July. He was going to go and watch some television for a while.

As soon as he turned it on, he saw that on the list of things to watch were more Christmas shows. Specials and cartoons were playing so that if you wanted to be in the mood for the holidays early, they had just the ticket. Turning it off, he went to the yard. There he shifted into his dragon and took to the skies.

He didn't even care that he'd left his good friend in his office without telling him where he was going. *Serves him right*, Noah thought. For making fun of him the way that he had. However, he knew he'd be back in his office in short order. Noah couldn't be rude to the man that had saved his life.

As he was landing in the yard, he stumbled and fell. "Did Dillon find himself a mate in Rankheart?" He was still thinking about that when he heard Devon's burst of laughter coming from the kitchen. "Bastard." But he loved him and could forgive his good friend of anything. Going into the kitchen, he was happy to see that more scones were being baked, and they were berries—his favorite.

Actually, any kind was his favorite, hot out of the oven. But he knew Bryce wouldn't allow someone to take the ones he loved the most. So while he munched on his warm buttered scone with his cup of hot tea, he told Devon what he'd been able to find out. Which, now that he thought on it, was a lot more than he'd first thought.

Chapter 8

Connor had plenty to work on, but he just couldn't stop thinking of the things he'd been able to find out from some of the ghosts that had checked in today. Dragons. They'd found a great many dragons, as well as a lot of dragon slayers. Even in death, they were a group that needed to be taken care of. He looked over at Roxanna when she cleared her throat. She'd been keeping him on track for the last hour or so.

"Right. Now, you said you needed to speak to your family regarding the box you planted in your yard." Roxanna told him that was the last case. "Yes, I remember now. You're here because...." Trailing off, he had hoped that someone would help him out. There was just too much on his mind today to be able to sit here and take care of business.

"I'm here on account'a I've been wanting to bag me

a dragon since I was a wee tot. Now that you've found them all and they be running around like there ain't nothing wrong with it, I think we should be able to have us some fun." Connor told him that he and the dragon were both dead; how much fun could it be. "It's a damn sight better than just leaning against the post hereabouts waiting for someone to come along that you might know to talk to. Don't you think?"

The dragons, ones that could fit into the shelter where they were, nodded as well. Connor asked Roxanna what he'd missed. There had to be something because the dragons would not have just agreed to let the hunters hunt them down in death as well.

"They can't die. I mean, it's a given fact that someone or something can't die twice. And the men and women here were warriors at one time. I think it would be fun to have them let off a bit of steam while they await their turn in line. You have to admit, there isn't any reason at all that we shouldn't allow them to have some fun." He laughed when she smiled at him. "Who knows. We might well have some fun watching them ourselves."

It was decided. The dragons that had come to put information in the book and the warriors that fought them were given permission to play in the skies. The best part was, no human could see them fighting, so there wouldn't be panic. And even the other family members came out to enjoy the show. Connor would never understand the dead. But then, he'd been having to deal with them for a very long time to make sure that things were right in their world.

After they were finished up for the day, he and Roxanna sat in the yard and watched the swordplay. It was exciting to see that they didn't just pretend their wounds when either side died. Dragons would fall to the ground, even falling over homes and businesses that were there. Also, they'd make noises he'd not ever heard, screams of pain, and then the loud laughter when one of them scored a hit on the warriors trying to fell them. After a while, the rest of them joined them on the lawn.

"Was it like this all those years ago?" It was Susanna that answered Ryan. She said it had been much worse. "I would imagine that when one of them fell from the sky like this, there were a great deal of deaths from that as well."

"It wasn't so much the deaths, but the aftermath of one falling from the sky. You have to remember that we're talking tonnage of weight just dropping and hitting the solid ground. There were others, wives and children, waiting there for one of us to fall so they could be the first to take what they could from the bodies." Susanna smiled sadly. "The stench was the worst. Decaying bodies of not just the dragons, but the people that would be killed. There was no end to the way they tried to hunt out our breeding places and destroy our children's eggs. It amazes me all the time that humans could go from trusting us to be there for them to killing so many of us that there are a scant few of us left. I know it seems like we have a lot of dragons now, but when people say the sky was darkened by them flying overhead, they aren't kidding."

"What did you do for the humans? I mean, you're terribly big as a dragon. How did the first human approach one of you to ask for help?" Ryan laughed at her own question. "I guess I'm imagining they sent this frightened young virgin to stand up to one of you to talk about the help."

"It was pretty much like that. But they would send children, children who had lost their parents for one reason or another. The dragons helped the humans with their crops and fields. The faeries told us that a dragon's poop is very high in nutrients." They all laughed with Susanna. "Then it seemed that someone decided an entire village could eat off a single dragon for a very long time. What they didn't know and found out too late was that dragon meat isn't all that good. It's stringy and tough. Mostly because it's primarily muscle."

"How did it become known that the parts of a dragon are magical? I mean, other than the fact that they could fly." Rylie had only just joined the family a few minutes into Susanna's discussion. "I'm sorry if you've already answered that."

"I haven't, and it's a great question. But as you pointed out, we could fly, and with our weight, it could have only been magic that held us up so well. I don't remember if it was a single family or a village, but it was discovered that once they started to bring parts of us into their homes — scales for their roofs, claws for digging, things like that — they started to get healthier. And with the scales being used, there was also a breeding increase. Anyone that touches a scale will be more fertile. There were other things as well that clued them in. Then along came a witch, and she began testing what she could find from a dragon in her brews or potions. After that, it became a free for all in everyone wanting a piece of them. The sale of our bodies was worth more to them than the friendship of a large animal that had worked beside them for all those years."

Some of the ghosts that had been play acting with the dragons joined them in the stories. The man that had started talking said he'd been killed by his own wife when she wanted to sell their roof right off the house so they'd have some coins. Another told of his brother turning him in to the police for hoarding dragon parts.

"I did nothing of the kind. But once it got out there, people believed what they wanted, I guess." The man laughed as he continued. "But I did me a good one before I passed. I handed off a scale to his missus, and they had a powerful bunch of children. All of them girls."

Everyone had a story or something to add to what they were talking about. It was like having a lesson from the ones that were there at the time. Better than any history class that Connor had ever been in. None of the human ghosts wanted glamour to make their wounds disappear but wore them like the battle scars they were. Connor thought he enjoyed that, the pride on their faces when they spoke of how they got whatever had felled them.

The dragons were no less proud of their marks. Most of them couldn't shift into a human, so it was Devon that did the translation when it was necessary, and they wanted to add something to the conversation. Noah had never thought of how much the dragons had suffered too. Not enough food. Forever being chased and killed. Their children sacrificed for the money they could bring. Even the waterways that some of them could feed from were not enough to feed their hunger.

"I wish we'd not touched them." One of them asked the newcomer why he'd say that. "Aye, you'd think I'd be the first to tell you I wish them all dead. But I missed the help when it came to planting and harvesting. I was so busy chasing that next dragon that I forgot me own duties to my family. They starved because of me."

"I'm so sorry. That must have been terrible for you." Cole took Ryan's hand when she spoke to the younger man. "Do you get to see them on this side?"

"Nay, I don't be looking for them. When they died, it was my fault, and I don't think I could take the look in their eyes when they'd only just begged me for food that morn. I left them there, with the promise of coming home with enough coin that we'd buy us a cow." He looked so sad that Noah could almost feel sorry for him. But as the man said, he'd been the one that had left them there without food or money. "I will stay on this side so as not to bother them. I don't deserve to be around good folk like my family was."

Walking back to his home, he and Roxanna talked about how their day had gone and how glad he was that she told him to let the dragons play. If nothing else had come from allowing them to burn off some steam, they had learned a great deal about the time when there were more than now. Connor did wonder what they were going to do about all the wisps that had been found. Thousands was much more than he thought it to ever be.

Their home was finished, and now as warm as any home he'd ever been in. There were parts of them both there, little things the two of them had picked up in their travels. As soon as they were able to, they'd start filling out the yard. Flowers for the faeries and others. Trees for the fruit. Connor thought he'd had the best life ever since meeting his Roxanna. He was going to spend every day telling her how much he needed and loved her because it was the truth.

"I've been thinking about what we witnessed today. I think this would be a great opportunity to write a book." He asked her if she was already bored with being his mate. "You know I'm not. But there is a great deal of history here. Not just with the dragons, but with the people that lived and died during that time. But instead of making it a history book, I'd make it some sort of romance. Magic galore."

"You'd have to have permission from Devon to write about dragons. I don't know that he'd say no, but he might have a good reason if he were to tell you to write about the people instead of men." She asked him about birds. "Birds? I don't understand. Did you hear something about dragon birds?"

"No. That's just silly. I was thinking of a castle that was being defended by birds. Larger than life birds that would only work with one king. No, she'd have to be their queen. I don't think a man would want to have birds around him. They seem so delicate. But these birds, my birds, would be loyal to only her and the people there." Roxanna squeaked. "Can you see them? Flying through the air? I know it was dragons that did, but in order to make it so that no one would be hunting us down, we'd make it about birds. Oh, Connor, I can almost see it all working out in my head already."

As she told him what she was thinking about, he could almost see it happening. A group of birds. The people from the time period they'd been witness to tonight. She told him of great ships and of hoarding food. Roxanna even thought she'd put some of the downsides to living during that time.

"Castle. I will need for her to have a big castle. A keep as well." Roxanna was so excited that he was too. "I don't know what I'll call it yet, but I'm going to start on it as soon as possible. This will be epic, don't you think? Romance in the skies. A castle with a queen. I'll have to figure out a reason that there is no king, but that shouldn't be too hard. Men during that time were pretty stupid. Going off leaving their family alone while they played at fighting? Why, I ask you? For more dirt that they could— I'm getting off track here. I'm going to start taking notes on my thoughts right now."

When she left him in the living room, he laughed. Christ, she was going to be good at this. It might not sell well, or it might sell out, but he doubted she'd care. It would be fun for her to write it, and Connor wanted her happy more than anything. Connor did wonder what Devon and the others would say about her big birds. How the hell would that even work?

She'd get it worked out; of that, he had no doubt. And it would be a good book, despite having large birds doing all the heavy work. When she came back to him, kissing him on the mouth as she moved by him, she was talking about birds of prey, falcons and even owls. He didn't even point out to her that owls and falcons weren't all that small in the first place.

Laughing with her, he sat down on the couch. When she handed him a sheet of paper, he looked it over. An outline. She had already fixed an outline of the story. Connor just shook his head and turned the television on. Not long after that, the two of them were brought tea and cakes. Connor decided that life was good.

~*~

Jackson looked over the list of wisps he'd been given. He'd not known that warrior dragons could depart from their bodies before they died, provided there was enough time—meaning they'd have to be dying when they did it, and not dead. It only worked about half the time, he'd been told, but that was enough for him to have a list of the original owners of all the dragons that had once been. Once he'd been able to count the names, he had the number closer to three hundred rather than thousands. He'd not thought of Rankheart not being able to count.

"So what happens to them now? I'm assuming that like Kelly, they'll go to someone worthy?" Jackson told Nicole that the wisps would make the choice as to who they thought worthy of being a dragon. "Oh, I didn't know that. So whoever they think is worthy of being a dragon, that's where they'll go? I like that. You'd not want just any person to be able to be a giant dragon whenever they were pissed off."

"Right. Rankheart has been watching over them for all these years, so she's ready to give them over to me to see to. Devon has so much on his plate right now that he's asked if we'd take this job. If you have other things to do, I can handle this." She told him they were both the dragon protectors. "I know, but I also know you're into about fifty other things with the other women."

"I've got this with you. I really don't think there is much we can do is there? I mean, if they pick out their host, that's about all there is to it. Or am I missing something?" He told her he doubted she missed much. "Very funny. If you want me to jump your bones, you only have to say so. There isn't any reason for you to butter me up."

"I'd love to butter you up. Cover you from head to toe in butter and slide my naked body over you." He started to reach for her, then there was a knock at the office door. "Whoever that is, they're not going to be long for this world. I can promise you that."

Rankheart came into the room when he bid her enter. The pixie hadn't been around much. None of them knew if she was living with Dillon, who they've not seen much of either, or if she was back in the caves she'd been in. When she asked permission to sit, it was Nicole that told her they were all family here.

"I've a question for you. Lord Devon said I was to come to you about it if it had anything to do with the wisps. It doesn't really, but he is so cranky I decided even if it didn't, I wasn't going to bother him." Jackson told Rankheart that it was more than likely a good idea. "I have their money. All of the wisps. They led me to their hiding places, and I brought it back with me to the cave. It's hidden deep within, so no one will find it. Also, I was able to ward it so that not just any creature could go inside where it is."

"Is there a great deal of it?" He almost regretted asking her that about sums of things, but she said it would not fit into the room they were in. "Mostly gems, I'm assuming?"

"Aye. They gave it to me. I don't think they realized that watching over them was payment enough for keeping them safe. But I nary spent any of it. I never took a single coin out of there." When he told her he believed her, she seemed to settle down again. Her anger at someone thinking she might well have made off with it was palatable. "There is mostly gems, yes. But when I came across something that was left behind, I brought it along with me too. Swords and the like. There are a few pieces of armor as well. Most of them I've cleaned up and oiled, so they're in good shape."

"You've preserved them?" She just shrugged.

Dillon came into the office with them, and he could see that the two of them were already in love. The pixie, being what she was, glowed with the newfound love. Dillon looked as if he might well be able to walk on air; he was so happy.

"What do you want to do with all the riches, Rankheart? I know you said you didn't take any of it, but I think you should take some of it as your own."

"Don't need it. I'm not without funds. My family, they were tight as a fisted monkey with his food when it came to spending. When they were murdered, too, I just brought my things to the cave where I was and kept an eye on that as well. Dillon and I, we don't want to do a regular job, but to watch over the wisps. The house that he had, I can make it safe for them. Dillon can do it too, now that I've shared with him." Rankheart glared at him again. "You canna take us apart after all I've done for the king."

"I'd never even think of such a thing. No, you and Dillon can watch over them. Dillon is working for us." He looked over at the besotted man. "Do you wish to stop working for us as our investor? It's all right if you'd like to stop, Dillon. You have a mate now, and that's more important than investing for us."

"I want to do both. That is if it's all the same to you guys. As Heart said, we can work from our home in keeping them safe. There doesn't seem to be too much work involved in the job, from what I can tell. They just need sunlight and fresh air. We have plenty of both." He grinned at him when Jackson asked him if he was sure. "I've never been more sure about anything in my life. Heart and I, we've got a lot of catching up to do in loving one another. And I do. Love her. I never in my life thought that love was like this. But I have it now, and I want to devote as much of my life as possible to seeing if there is a way of making more. Happiness, I mean."

Jackson loved what he was saying. It didn't sound sappy or anything. He was sure that Dillon meant every word of what he said, too. But there was still the matter of the gems and other items. He made himself a note to ask Devon about it.

"I've had them separated out. Each wisp has its own

section of things that I've found for them. I have to tell you that there are a few that never stayed with us. It was too much, I think, for some to be without a dragon. Did you know that they can kill themselves?" Jackson told her he'd not even known about wisps until now. "I guess they like to keep that part of themselves quiet. I know I would. But it's possible. They only have to go into a living body that can't handle the power given to them. It's usually a human on the verge of dying anyway. I don't know that they do it every time, but the passing of the human is so much easier with the last of their magic."

"You have taken a great deal of time and energy in caring for them, haven't you?" Again Heart, as she was now going to be called, he supposed, only shrugged Nicole off. "Whatever is left behind from those that died, you and Dillon must take it. If you don't need it, then you can set up some kind of fund for others that might. Such as college funds or something along those lines. We owe you so much, Heart. More than I think any of us realize."

"I was just doing what I should be doing." She looked over at Dillon. "I think I got more than even the money can bring me. I've a good man that is happy with me. He don't care none if I can't cook. I canna slay his dragon either."

"Wait. What?" Heart asked him what he was talking about. "Dillon has a dragon? When did this happen? Was it one of the wisps that I have on my list here? I'm not angry, please don't take it like that. I'm actually thrilled beyond words that he has one of them. Did you get one too?"

"Nay. I've no need for one. I have my own." They both stood up, and she looked at him. "I'll be with the wisps if you've a mind to allow me to do that. Also, when you're ready to take their gems, I'll help you with that. There is a bit and some there. It's not going to be disturbed."

"And the other? The coins that won't be claimed? What will you do with that? You don't need to tell me now, Heart, but I know Devon will want you to have it." She told him she'd think on it. "Good. That's better than telling me no."

"Ha. If I had a told you no, then that would have been all right with you too. I'm not one to trifle with. When I tell you something, my word is my bond. If I decide to take the coins, I'll do something with it to make those that left them behind proud." Nicole told her she didn't doubt that one bit. "Thank you. Dillon and I are going to meet up with his sisters now. They've got some magic too with me being his mate."

When they simply disappeared, Jackson looked over at Nicole. "I think she just threatened me." Nicole said he didn't need to think on it, that she had indeed threatened him. "I don't know why, but I have a feeling I should take her word for it. That she could cause me a world of hurt the likes of which I've never seen before."

"I've no doubt. But there is something I don't think

any of you noticed about Heart. When Devon first told us about her, he called her Rankheart the Red. She said it was for all the blood she shed. Then today, she was sporting a different head crown than she was before. This one is larger and more ornate. I believe Dillon has one as well, but he's not had it on here. He had the marks of wearing one on his head." Jackson asked her if she thought them royalty. "I do. She's not one to brag, I think, and Dillon is very backward. But I'd bet anything, especially after she said her family was all dead, that she and Dillon are the royalty of the pixies in some way. I don't know how far up they go, but I'd say if they're not the king and queen, then they're very close to being them."

"Well, what do you think of that?" He looked where the two of them had been sitting. "Now that you mention it, I did see that her crown was larger. I think I was simply caught up in what she was saying to us. Dillon as king? The man can barely put two words together most of the time. I think he'll make a great king if the way he spoke about his love for Heart is any indication."

"I love you that much. I honestly do." Jackson said she made his heart leap with joy by saying that. "You're such a sap. I think I might have said that to you before."

He chased her out of his office and then sat down to call Devon. He had his notes, and he wanted to make sure he didn't leave anything out when talking to him. Jackson knew he was leaving himself open to Devon finding him something else to do, but he didn't care. Just having one of them take over the task was something he was forever grateful for. Also, he wanted to figure out what sort of promotion Dillon had gotten.

Jackson liked the younger man. He had gone through hell and back and had come out on top. Not that he didn't suffer at the hands of Sandra. He had, greatly so. But now he was in love, an emotion that seemed to suit him. Picking up the phone, Jackson was glad that Devon seemed to be in a much better mood than he had been. This morning when he called there, Devon had nearly bitten his head off. He wondered what had changed him.

"I'm sorry about this morning." Jackson thought it was the perfect time to get the answer to the question he'd just asked himself. "Do you remember me telling you, a very long time ago, about the buildings that had to come down in the States? Grandmother and I own them in a partnership to help with the preservation of the buildings in the main capital area. Well, I got a late call this morning telling us that the buildings had been torn down in an effort to make more parking. Of course, I blew my top, and that didn't go over well. So, they're refunding me all the money I would have sold them for had I wanted. I doubt very much that they realize how much I paid for them back in the day, nor how much they're worth now. Anyway, I'm sorry. Your call couldn't have been timed any worse."

After telling him everything he'd found out about the wisps, Jackson told him about Dillon and the gems

Heart was going to watch over. Devon was laughing as he finished up. Jackson asked him what he thought was so funny.

"I don't know. We have such an array of different magic now that it wouldn't surprise me if she were the queen of all pixies. And that she and Dillon will have a million children to repopulate the world with them. What does a pixie do, anyway? I'm going to ask my grandma. She'll know." She would too, Jackson thought. "I do remember someone telling me once that they're very mischievous and cause trouble. Maybe that's just what Dillon needs. Someone to get him into trouble once in a while. I'll get back with you on it when I speak to my grandma. Thanks for letting me know. And you're right; whatever she or Dillon want out of the stash, it's theirs. She should have been paid for her part in keeping them safe, and I can't think of anything better than her taking it as she needs it."

Jackson decided he'd hold off telling either one of them of the decree that Devon had laid down, stating that the money and stash they guarded would be theirs forevermore. Dillon might well be all right with it, but the pixie was still getting to know them. He'd just wait until the time was right. Jackson did wonder how many decades would go by before he found the right time.

After finishing up on his work for the day, Jackson went to find his beautiful mate. She had mentioned that she wanted to do some work in the yard earlier. Perhaps he'd take her on top of the mountain again, one of their favorite places to make love, and have a picnic with her. In addition to making love, he was going to try and convince her to stay up there with him all night. Jackson could not wait to see what the next fifty years or so would bring them all. He was looking forward to everything they encountered. So long as he had Nicole at his side.

Chapter 9

Noah wasn't sure what to do with all his time. Bryce and her grandma, as well as her mom, had gone on a hunting trip. Unlike some hunting trips he'd heard of, the three of them were looking for plants they could bring to their own gardens. He'd always thought it a joke when witches would find herbs and such to make spells. But Grandma Bee was somewhat old fashioned in some ways. She loved to make up potions that she could sell to the humans.

"It's not anything that will harm them. I do put a little magic in them to make sure the people are feeling more up. Humans can take so many things the wrong way anymore. I put a little cheer in my things so they'll at least have a good few hours." He asked her if she did that to him. "My goodness, Noah. If you got any happier, I think you'd burst. I would have thought having all these women under your feet all the time, you'd be having a fit."

"But I love all of my women." She winked at him. "I'm especially in love with my mate. She lets me sleep with her."

"You stinker." She had laughed about what he'd said to her up until they left. Then she took him aside to speak to him. "I want you to have those lovely faeries do me a favor. Can you have them bring us some blossoms? I don't care what they bring to the kitchen, just so long as I can crush them up into some flavors for my potions. I'm thinking of making some lovely lotions for my shop."

"You know they won't mind that at all. But why are you telling me like this? I mean, usually, you shout to the world what you need me to do." She giggled, and he smiled at her. "I'm not sure you're aware of what that little laugh does to a man. It makes him feel like he should slay something for you."

"You always have the perfect thing to say when I need it. I'm making some of the pretty things for Laura. You know that her and Austin spoke last night well into the morning. She's a little down. I thought the two of us could work on it together." Austin was Grandma Bee's son, Bryce's father. He'd been killed a long time ago when Bryce had been just a little girl. But he could come and visit them thanks to Roxanna. "She's already made me enough jams and jellies to sell that I think she needs to change things up a little. I want to help her."

"You know they'll do whatever you want them to do. But I'll have you some blooms here when you return. You will return, right?" He laughed when she did. "I love you guys, so have some fun."

That had been yesterday. They were set to come home tomorrow. He hadn't realized how much he depended on someone to be there when he was in the house. No wonderful smells were coming from the kitchen. No women's laughter that simply made him smile to hear it. But he missed most of all the way they would brighten up a room like a tree did at Christmas time. He really did love these women.

Going into the dining room, he was about to back out when he saw what the faeries had been up to. But as soon as one of them saw him, he was caught. Going into the room, he could only stare in amazement at all the flowers they'd found for Bee.

"She'll be surprised, don't you think?" He nodded, unsure of how to tell Maggie that she hadn't wanted a room full of them. "I know it's a lot of blooms. Whatever she doesn't take, we'll use them to dry for seeds. We went a little overboard."

"Yes, I can see that. But you can use them, so they won't go to waste." They had separated them into different baskets. Bushel baskets of them were even hanging from the ceiling, covering the floor, as well as simply hanging in the open air. "Are you guys still bringing them in?"

In answer to his question, three faeries came into

the room and went to the only section of the room that wasn't filled — under the table. While he watched, they put several different piles of the blooms there and left the room again. He wasn't going to tell them to stop — let them have some fun. He looked at Maggie.

"What do you know about the containers that Grandma Bee uses? You know, to put her things in for the shop she and Lady Laura have?" She said that the faeries had made them for her. "I'm not saying you should fill a room with them, but I know she's going to need more jars with lids. Also, I know each of you put a little magic on the things you help her with, so I'm asking you to put a little happiness in the ones that Lady Laura takes home with her."

"We saw that she was sad today. Even going on this trip, she wasn't as happy as we had wished." Noah told her that was one of the reasons for the flowers. "Oh, what a wonderful idea. She will have the best. Also, your lordship, we were wondering if we could go into the shop and spruce it up for the weekend. There are so many things we can do while they're gone."

"Yes, well, I'd ask Bryce about that. You do remember what happened when you tried to spruce up her car?" Maggie nodded and told him again they were sorry. "I know you didn't mean any harm, but to have her entire car decorated from top to bottom, including the wheels, was just too much. Try and temper what you do with a little bit of that in mind."

He knew as soon as she left him that it was going to be over the top. It was like everything they did for someone—too much never entered their minds. And over the top was the only thing they knew. Noah still found himself laughing about when Bryce had sent him a picture of the car they'd worked on for her. It was literally covered from the hood of the car to all the way around the wheels in flowers. Not only that, but the inside was made up the same way. Even to this day, they were still finding flower petals when they got in. And it reeked of flowers.

Noah was headed out back to take a fly-by when Cole pulled into the yard. He and Ryan had been helping with the book Roxanna was writing, and he told Noah that he needed a break. Before he could tell him what he was doing, someone pulled into the drive behind him. Neither of them knew who the stranger was.

"I'm looking for Bryce Frost. I was told that she lived here." Neither him nor Cole answered the man. "I see. Tight-lipped, are you? Well, I have some money for her. Does that loosen your tongues?"

"Who are you, and who is it you're looking for again? We didn't catch your name in all that." The man put out his hand, and Cole, who was closer, ignored it. "Putting your hand out for me to snatch off isn't going to win you any brownie points. Answer the question, please."

"Howard Kerby. I'm looking for Bryce because I have some money for her. It's quite a sum of money too. Can you please tell me if she lives here or not?" Cole pointed out that Kerby had said he'd already been told that she lived there. "I'm looking for her so I can talk to her."

"Talk to her or give her money? What is it you're doing here, Mr. Kerby? And don't lie to me again." The man was fighting hard with the compulsion, and Noah had to laugh a little. "What is your name? Why are you looking for a woman named Bryce Frost?"

"My name is Howard Kerby. I'm looking for a woman by the name of Frost because I've heard that she's a witch of some repute. I think interviewing her would put my story on the front page of every paper in the world." The man fought harder than before in not answering Cole. "She's been helping women around the area for years, and I want to know what she puts in her lotions that make it so people are too fucking happy."

"So, you're trying very hard not to tell us that you think your wife got some of her things if she indeed does that sort of thing, and it made her happy all the time. Why does that bother you so much?" Cole turned and winked at him, and Noah sat down on the front steps to watch this unfold. He'd forgotten that at one time, Cole had been a cop. "I think having a happy wife is the greatest gift in the world. But then that might just be me."

"She's fucking happy all the fucking time now. And I can't get her upset." Cole asked him why he'd want to do that to his wife. "Nobody should be that fucking happy. She sings too. Do you know how annoying that is to hear someone whistling all the time? Yesterday I told her I'd lost my job. You know what she did? She told me I'd get another one. Or, and I want you to know this too, while she was smiling like a loon, she told me that either I got myself a job or she'd toss me out. In that fucking sing song voice she has."

Cole laughed with him. Noah was having a lot of fun over this man's misfortune of having a happy wife. Cole finally asked the man why he thought this Frost person had anything to do with it. Mr. Kerby ran his hands through his hair, something it looked as if he had been doing a great deal, and told him he just needed for her to stop selling the shit to her.

"Did it ever occur to you that your wife is just simply happy?" Kerby said again that no one was that happy. "Then perhaps it's you. That your sour mood is making her try and make up for the fact that you're nothing but a sour puss. Are you?"

"You're confusing me." Cole just stood there. "Are you going to tell me if she lives here or not? I have to find this woman. I'm going to give her all the money I have and tell her not to sell it to my wife again. That's not right that she's doing it in the first place."

"Perhaps you should find whatever it is you swear is making your wife happy and use a little on yourself." Kerby just stared at Cole. "Couldn't hurt, you know. Besides, you might like having a smile on your face once in a while. I'm sure it'll take some practice on your part."

Cole came up and sat down on the steps while Kerby just stood there. "You're not going to help me, are you?" Cole told him that they had. That if he couldn't stand his wife singing, he should join her. "That's not what I want."

"I guess it just sucks to be you then. You'd better be finding a job, however. I don't think, since she's so happy all the time now that Mrs. Kerby is going to stand for you to be unemployed. I'd think on that really hard if I were you. You should go to a few of the places in town that have help wanted signs on the door."

"You're a right bastard, you know that? I don't know what the big deal is for you to tell me where this woman lives. Christ, you'd think it was some sort of national secret or something."

Kerby stood there for several more minutes, then finally got into his car. As he drove by the two of them sitting on the porch, he flipped them off.

"Well, that was certainly entertaining." They both sat there and laughed until Noah told him he was going out to have himself a little flight time. As they went to the back yard, they talked about having faeries in the house. "You should see the flowers the women are going to come home to. I don't think it will be anytime soon that Bee asks them to gather things for her again."

Shifting and taking to the skies, they said very little to each other. Flying was something that Noah didn't do all that often, and he decided he'd make sure he tried to do it more often. It was relaxing. Not to mention, he could empty his mind of all his worries while up here. As a dragon, Noah knew that all problems would just be too small for him to worry over.

After another hour of being in the sky, they both landed on the ground in his back yard. Noah invited Cole to dinner, but he declined. He told Noah that the only reason he'd come over in the first place to see if he wanted to take a flight with him.

"I need to get going anyway. I have several things going that I have no desire to finish up." Noah asked Cole why not. "That will mean I don't have anything to do tomorrow. Having Dillon around to do the things we all had a hand in is taking away from what I used to do. Not that I want the job back, but I have to figure out something for me to do that takes up some time. I never thought I'd say this, but I'm bored not having a job."

"I know just what you mean. I'm jealous of the women. They have an agenda that keeps them going all the time. You know, finding things to make and put into a shop. I need something like that." Cole cocked his head at him like he had just thought of something. "What is it? Whatever it is, I want in on it."

"We've been bitching for months now about the shit we've accumulated in the big warehouse. It's doubtful to me that any of us want whatever is left in there. I know for a fact that I'm not going to take it. There are four empty buildings side by side, just off Main Street. What do you think about dragging all that shit there and selling it off? Hell, if it needs to be cleaned up, we can do that too." Noah loved that idea and told him he did. "We could make a little money on it and put it towards one of the million charities that we have our hands in. The last time I was in there, I saw that even Heart had put some of the things in there from her parents' home. I could care less if we didn't make a dime so long as we have a place to go every day. What do you say?"

Before either of them could change their mind, they went to the four buildings. Sure enough, someone at one time had connected the four of them, and that was when they hit on the idea of setting up each room with a different time period. Noah thought they could keep the place fresh all the time with the amount of shit just the two of them had.

The clean up was done by the time they were bringing over the first truckload of stuff. The faeries, it seemed, were as bored as they were and cleaned the buildings from top to bottom in less time than it had taken them to pick out a room for the stuff. Even after unloading the things they'd deemed good enough to start with, the faeries had brought over some of the other pieces. Christ, they were going to have fun with this; Noah just knew it.

By the time Bryce and her grandma and mom joined them, they were well on their way to having two of the rooms set up. After telling the faeries their plan of keeping one room for each different time period, they would bring those things over for them. He could tell that Bryce loved it when she squealed like she did when she figured out a new spell. Noah was just happy to have someone taking it seriously. He'd been worried about that.

They hadn't been home yet. Noah had hoped they'd see the dining room before he got back. But they decided to have dinner in town and then look over the other things that were still in the warehouse. Christ, Noah thought, this was going to keep him busy for a while. At least he hoped so.

~*~

Matthew stared at Honey for a few minutes before it sank in as to what she was telling him. Shaking his head, he was almost afraid to have her repeat herself again. She was getting fussy with him. Leaning back on his hands, he asked her to tell him once again what she'd come to see him for.

"Are you going to listen this time? My lord." She added that last bit because she wanted to let him know how mad she was at him. "I'm sure that what I have told you three times now is considered old news and should be updated by now. They are finished with the panels that you found in the warehouse yesterday. They are not the ones you thought them to be."

"The panels were the only ones in the place. How can they not be the ones I'm looking for?" She growled at him. "I'm not asking you, Honey. I'm speaking to myself. I so wanted those to be put into the nursery I was planning to surprise Aisling with. Why are you so sure they're not the ones I wanted?"

"They have naked women on them, sir. A naked man too, but he is...he is with all the women." Now he remembered the panel. "The one you told us to look for and to clean up was supposed to have had babies on it. Not the act of making them."

Matthew laughed, which didn't make Honey any happier with him. "Perhaps that was what I was thinking. That the panels had ideas on making babies." He laughed when she pinked up in anger. "Take that one to the shop Noah is working on. Might as well see if we can make a few coins from it while it's cleaned up. What do you say?"

"I say that should you see this thing, you'd want it destroyed. It is the most obscene thing I've ever seen." He didn't bother reminding her that it had been made in a different time, and more than likely would have been in some very wealthy man's mistress's bedroom. "I shall take it to the shop and let them deal with it. I should never want to see that again."

"Don't be a prude, Honey. I honestly didn't remember there might be more than one of those things I was looking for." She nodded and sat down on his leg. "I'm glad they're cleaning the place out. I'm sure that over the next few centuries, we'll be filling it out again. There is nothing wrong with keeping things to share but to keep them because you hate to see them go to waste is another thing entirely. They've become waste anyway."

"Did you know that the ladies of the houses are making sure we have enough material to make our homes warmer? Just yesterday, there was a large stack of scraps of cloth put out that we can have. I've never seen such colors." He told her he'd heard that was happening. "And glass too. Bits of it so we can put colorful windows in our own homes. I have two doors now that are colorful and bright."

"Aisling was telling me there are places that are giving them the wood they can no longer use in their places of business. All sorts of lengths and widths that can be made into anything you need." He'd heard about the flowers too. That had him laughing at the oddest times. "Do you suppose the seeds that were ordered from the catalog are as good as the ones that you guys saved up? I don't mean to imply that they're of better quality than yours, but just a curious question for you."

"They're not of superior quality, no. But now that we have seeds to work with, or even saplings to grow again, we can give them the boost they need to make sure they're as good as the ones we've lost. The gardens will be fuller this year from the hunting that Lady Bryce and her family has done for us. The seed drier is a good thing to have. No longer will we have to wait for days on end to make a batch that can be put into bags to store. What do you know of gems, my lord?" He asked her what she meant. Their worth? What they were called? "Their worth. I was only to ask you about them then say no more. But I don't think this is a good thing to leave unanswered. Understand?"

"No. Not really. Did someone ask you to ask me about gems' worth? Or are you asking because you don't know?" She told him she'd found some, with another faerie. "Where did you find them, Honey? I mean, were they, you think, the stash of another dragon?"

"I don't believe so. They are marking the walls to a great deep tunnel below the mountain beyond. They're not piled up as a dragon would do, but some are still within the walls. Others are just lying about in the water there. The mountain that you and Lady Aisling have picnics at." He nodded, wondering whether, if the faeries knew they were there having a picnic, did they also know that they made love quite often up there? "There is a small opening, small enough for only one of us to enter. Patrick and I were mushroom hunting, and we entered there when the rains came. Being curious, we followed the tunnel to an opening on the other end. It's larger there, but still not big enough for a man to walk through."

"What sort of gems did you find?" She told him. "Diamonds are very expensive. But if there are a great many of them, you wouldn't bring them out all at once. They'll be worth less if you were to do that. Did you and Patrick have an idea what you were going to use the gems for?"

"You'd not take them from us?" Matthew thought this was why she'd brought it up. He told her he'd not found them; she had. "Patrick said you'd want them for yourself. I think that I shan't be with him anymore as a friend. He has been telling everyone that he will be rich someday. What use does a faerie have to be rich? He cannot even turn bigger like you."

"Greed? I'm not sure if I know Patrick or not, so I have no way of knowing his mind. But I'd never take anything from you, Honey. You and he found the gems, and I feel they're yours to keep and do with what you wish. If you need help getting them out of the mountain, it would be my pleasure to help you with that."

"I thought you would say that. Despite what Patrick thinks." He waited for her to say more. There were rules she'd have to follow if she and Patrick were to bring the gems out of the mountain. "I'm going to go to the lady of the earth to allow her to tell us what to do with such a treasure. I think Patrick will be most upset with me, but I'm fearful of doing the wrong thing with them. Talking to you, has made me feel stronger about talking to her."

"Are you afraid of the lady of the earth, Honey?" She nodded and looked around as if she might sneak up on them. "I know for a fact that she's a fair and wonderful person. She might well know that the gems are there. I would think, and this is just my opinion, that you should allow her to tell you if they belong to another. Or if she knows of them being there, and will allow you and Patrick to bring them out."

"I will do that." She stood up and turned to look at him before flying away. "I will return shortly to tell you what she has said to me. But I would be happy too if you were to keep me safe should Patrick not like what I have done. He told me not to tell anyone, especially the lady. I am of a mind like you are. I do not wish to be in trouble over this."

Matthew got up from the ground and made his way to the lazy pond that was on his property. He had always wondered where in the mountain the waterway came from. Now he'd bet that it had something to do with the one Honey had found. Leaning over, he picked a small diamond out of the water and put it in his pocket. He'd been picking them up since the day he'd moved into this home. Matthew was nearly to his house when Patrick showed up.

"Where is she?" He asked the little creature who he was talking about. "Honey. She and I had an agreement, and now she's messed it all up. She wasn't to tell anyone what we have found."

"What is it you've found?" He backed from him, and Matthew saw the sword that was hanging on his side. "What have you in mind to do with that, Patrick? Hurt one of your own? Tell me."

"She said it would be ours to share, but I no longer trust her to share with me. If she is gone, then I can have it all to myself." Matthew made no move to indicate that the lady of the earth had joined them. Honey was with her. "If she is dead, I can have all the gems to myself."

"What would have been your plan with them? You cannot cash them in. They're deep in the stone, I was told." Patrick started cursing and swinging the blade that was now in his hand. "To harm a dragon is death, Patrick. You know that too. You put that away, and I won't have to harm you to save myself."

"You know too much." The blade came within an inch of his face. "You must die."

"*Stop.*" Patrick stopped swinging this blade at him. It took Matthew a moment to realize that it wasn't because he stopped by himself, but the lady had stopped him. When Patrick disappeared, Matthew bowed down on his knee before her. "He wished to harm you, Lord Matthew. I am sorry for that. I have only just spoken to Honey here on the gems she has found. I would like, with your permission, to leave them there. They are a fallback, I believe the humans call them, in the event that we need things from the human world."

"You need not worry over the gems at all, my lady. And if you were to need anything from the human world, you know that any one of us would get it for you." She told him to rise up. Matthew did so, and Honey came to land on his shoulder. "She was right in telling you all, I'm thinking."

"She was. I have rewarded her too. Honey will take

out as many gems as she can carry when she goes there and use them as she sees fit." The lady smiled. "She has told me of the things the ladies of the family are doing for them. She only wishes to make them a trinket for their help. I think that a splendid idea."

"I do, as well. It will be something they will treasure for a long time too." The lady looked at Honey and told her she was promoted to first faerie. That meant she'd have her own group of faeries that she would command. It was a great honor for anyone to receive. "Thank you for that, my lady. I did fear that I was overworking Honey. This way, she will be less stressed too."

After the lady left them, Honey stopped him from going into the house. She looked upset with something, and he asked her what was going on. When she bowed her head, he asked her to look at him.

"I got Patrick killed. My heart hurts from that." Matthew told her he'd done that all on his own when he'd tried to harm him. "But he wouldn't have done it had I not told."

"Do you think it was the right thing to do to tell on him?" She nodded. "Then you have nothing to feel guilty about, Honey. Had he not attacked me this way, I know he would have killed you given the chance. Even had you not told anyone, he would have let his greed of it justify killing you. You did the correct thing."

Matthew handed over the diamonds he'd been picking up. There were about two dozen of them. The two of them worked on the first bracelet of the ones she was going to make. Just before it was finished, Honey pulled out a larger ruby and fitted it in the middle of the chain.

"I think that to be perfect, my lord." Using her own magic, she linked the diamonds together to form a chain. "It will size itself for the wearer. I think too that I shall make it so that it never leaves their wrist. I believe they'd be much upset should they were to lose it. Don't you think?"

"I do. It's lovely. I know they'll each wear it with pride too." She thanked him and handed him the first bracelet. "You should give it to them. This will be much nicer coming from you."

"Nay, this one is for you, my lord. For saving my life and keeping me from being in trouble. For each of these diamonds, I love you triple their worth."

When she fitted it over his wrist, he felt the love and the magic that had gone into making it. Matthew was glad she'd given it to him.

Epilogue

Cole loved his family, especially when they were all able to get together like they were now. Well, not all of them, but the ones that had begun this journey in making a place for the dragons. He glanced over at his mate, who was swollen with their second child, seeing the sparkle of the bracelet that all the women and men wore, and wondered, as he did every hour of every day, how he'd gotten to be so lucky in having such a wonderful person as his mate. His son, Baxter, came to sit on the swing with him. He was nearly twelve now, his face filling out with muscle instead of baby fat. Cole was glad they'd waited twenty years to have children. It had given him the much needed time to see the world with Ryan. She winked at him as she chased after one of Dillon's children.

Now there was a man who had a lot of children. Devon had told him right after Dillon's fourth child had been born that he had predicted Dillon and Heart would have a lot of children. The two of them now had ten, five of each, none of them born singly, but in twos and threes. They'd all learned something when the children started coming around too. That pixies, unlike other small creatures, were born with wings and magic.

From their first breath, they could fly. Not only that, but they could most assuredly cause trouble by just being around the kids. Not really trouble, but it was sometimes the highlight of his day to see what they'd gotten into. Three of their children had been caught at one thing or another since they'd come into the world. Cole was glad that Dillon was a good father and seemed to have more patience than most. Heart simply loved them all.

Rylie and William had three little ones. The three of them that had lived had been born as fae. One, the last one they'd had, was born human and had died almost as soon as she'd been birthed. Cole didn't know who had taken her death harder, Rylie or her sister. William was heartbroken, but he held strong for his mate. Cole hoped never to have to go through what the two of them had. But rather than pulling them apart as it did humans, Cole thought they were all stronger for it. But every day, he could see that they were dealing with the loss of one so small.

They'd told him it was the power. No matter what they were born as the power of fae came to them. The little girl's body just couldn't handle such an overwhelming amount being given to her. Hugging his son when he said he was going to play with his cousins, he felt happy that his son was still happy to hug him when others were around.

"I have an idea that you're being sappy again." He asked Ryan why she'd think that as she sat down where Baxter had been sitting. "Just an idea. I get so worn out when just walking about anymore. It's like I'm carrying the weight of the world around my waist. Have you heard from Devon and Kelly?"

They had gone on a trip over a year ago. If anyone were to ask, it was just to see the world. But in reality, they'd made this special trip to go and see as many dragon clans as they could. Devon told him that he couldn't believe the conditions some of them were living in.

"Why aren't they making themselves gems to get into a better situation?" Devon told him he'd asked them the same thing. "I'm sure they think they have a really good answer for that. Tell me, is it because they're afraid of getting into trouble with you?"

At some point between the previous king and Devon, dragons had been told not to sell off their gems or any of their stash because that would bring the law down on their heads. Then the king would kill them. It had been difficult for Kelly and Devon at first, but as word spread that he wasn't going to kill anyone, the more places they visited, there was work going on to improve the lifestyle of the dragons he came upon.

The trip was coming to an end now, and they were expecting them to be home in the coming fall. Cole missed him a great deal. And Kelly. She was fun to be around, and her and Ryan, with the rest of the women, knew how to get things done.

"I've only heard that they're making their way back and will be here by Thanksgiving for sure. Then when they return, Dillon and Heart will be leaving for their other home." Dillon and Heart were the king and queen of the pixies. Every time they left, it felt like a huge hole was in his heart. "Thankfully, they'll only be gone for a few months instead of over a year. It's good that they can go there and work to come home to all of us."

Having Dillon around to hang out with was more fun than he'd had with any of the other dragons. They were brothers in all ways except for blood. They also worked on several projects together and enjoyed that as well. Even when Dillon was away, they kept in touch almost daily. Usually, it was work related, but more and more lately, it was just to check in with each other.

After Ryan said she was going to go and see to the children, he watched her as all the pixies came and landed on her shoulders and arms. They loved their aunt. However, Cole wasn't surprised when two of them, the little boys, came to sit with him on the swing. They stayed their little size as he rocked them gently.

"Girls are goofy. Why would they want to go and have tea when there is so much to do outside? I don't think I'll ever find me a mate. They take up too much of your time." Spoken like a true ten-year-old. That was another thing Cole had figured out. Children were children no matter what they were born as. "Uncle Cole, why did you want to have Aunt Ryan as a mate? Wasn't there, I don't know, somebody else that you'd rather have around? I know you can't marry a cousin or anything, but I'd sure like to be able to find me one that I can have fun with."

"I'm sure as you get older, you'll change your mind about that as well." Hal told him that he wasn't going to fall for that either. Women changing his mind on this. "I'm sure you've talked this over with your dad, right? What did he say to you about finding a mate."

"He said it would just hit you right between the eyes, and you'd wonder why you ever thought you could do without." Hal looked up at him. "It sounds like one of them mushy cards he buys for Mom. He buys her flowers too. Then she looks at him like he's a big peanut butter sandwich with marshmallows on it. I'm never gonna look at a girl like that. It's repulsive if you ask me."

Cole let his laughter go. Kids. He certainly did love hanging out with them. He learned so much from them that he wondered why someone didn't write a book. That had him thinking of the books his sister-in-law had been writing. She was a best seller, world known, and was having the best time of her life when she was asked to chair things in regard to her ability to write such wonderful stories. They all contributed to the books. It was, he thought, another family thing that they were all proud of.

The boys left him when he told them that love was the grandest emotion they'd ever experience. That it really did hit you between the eyes, and you'd never think of life again without having your mate by your side. Hal told him he'd rather get sick on his favorite sandwich than kiss a girl. Of course, that had Cole in tears; he was laughing so hard.

Cole kept an eye on his wife. She would overdo things, and he was worried for her. She would fuss at him if she knew that. He sort of liked it when she did that.

He saw Roxanna talking to someone, someone he was sure wasn't alive. Cole decided to join her when he saw that Connor was also busy with one of his *clients*, he called them.

Roxanna looked at him, and he could see that she was highly pissed. When he asked her if she needed his help, she surprised him by saying yes. Cole couldn't see the ghosts, not all the time unless they allowed it. The ghost that appeared in front of him as soon as she said yes looked like he'd been dead for some time.

"I want her to find my killer and kill her." Cole told the ghost that things didn't work that way. "I don't care how things work for others. I'm not going to be laying there rotting for another month. Find the fucker and then kill her. But make sure you put her body out where nobody can find her either."

"You've been given the rules upon your death, yes?" He only waved him off. All of them, all the family, knew the rules regarding the dead in the event Roxanna or Connor needed help. "Why do you think you should be exempt from having to follow the rules like everyone else? I mean, there isn't a section for assholes that I'm aware of. In the event you didn't understand me, that's what you're being right now."

"You're very funny. Giving a dead man a hard time. I should be exempt because I say so. It's not like I'm really dead anyway. We all know she can bring the dead back. That's what I want too, to be brought back so I can finish up on the things that are still in the works for me." He glared at Roxanna. "She said that's not the way it works. But I know better. I've seen it on television."

"You have? Well, hell. That makes it perfectly right then, doesn't it, Roxanna? He's seen it on television. The man is brilliant. I think you should just bring him back like they said." He put his finger to his mouth, then looked at the man while he pretended to be thinking about it. "However, so you know, you're already as back as you're going to get. I'd say you're about twenty-four hours from exploding, as a matter of fact."

"Why, you smart ass. I should knock you three ways from Sunday." Cole told him to go ahead and try. If he did, he was going to have Roxanna send him to White Land.

It's the place where the ghosts that weren't cooperating were sent. "You can't do that either. Want to know why? Because I'll have your job if you even look like you're going to do it. Fucking bitch. Go find my killer and do her in."

Cole was hit with the information on what had happened to the man. As he reran the reason he'd been killed and by who, he wanted to kill the man himself. Instead, he decided to just put the man in his place.

"Your wife is finally happy, and you aren't going to do a thing about it either. You beat her daily. Verbally and mentally abused her with every breath you took. She killed you when you tried to kill her with the gun you brought with you. The woman you forced to have an affair with you helped her. I think the two of them should be happy to be away from you." He thought of something else. "I'm going to make sure your body is never found. With a little magic, I can make it so that people and other creatures will walk over you without ever seeing what kind of piece of shit they're walking over."

He had no idea why he said that, but the images that came from the man's mind or memories — whatever they were — pissed Cole off so much that he wanted the man to suffer in some small way. He looked over at Roxanna, and she smiled at him. Cole was more confused than he'd been when the images came to him.

"Do it." He didn't say anything while standing in

front of the man. He was embarrassed enough. "You make it so the earth never gives him up, and I'm going to send him on to White Land."

The man was sent on. Cole told Roxanna what had happened and that he wasn't sure he knew how to do what he'd said. She smiled at him and then laughed. He asked her what she thought was so funny.

"You. It doesn't matter if his body is found or not. He'll never know about it. The body could be found within the next few minutes, but he'll never know. The threat alone is enough to have him suffering with the knowledge that he won't be found. I love that. I'm going to have to use that one again. Did you really see what he had done?" Cole nodded. "I've never seen what was in their head like that. Perhaps that was what led you over here in the first place. So that you could deal with him properly. Thank you for that."

After she gave him a hug, he went to find something else to do. He'd been sitting around long enough. Going by the food tables again, he made himself a plate of junky type food and found Ryan. He thought perhaps she'd been standing around too much today.

Laughing to himself, he thought about what she'd say if he told her to have a seat. When he got to her, she was laying on a large towel with two children, Connor's kids, and napping. Pulling up a chair, he watched her in slumber, the way he had every morning since the two of them moved into their home.

~*~

She watched the six men as they sat in the big room. They had come in here to watch the television. However, it was muted, and the remote was laying among the foods that had been brought in for the occasion. Their conversation was animated, sometimes loud and filled with laughter. Each time one of them laughed loudly, she would join them. Watching them, she wondered if anyone would know that there sat six of the most wealthy and powerful men in the world.

"You can talk to them, should you wish." Shaking her head at the newcomer, she told him it would be an awkward meeting. "I doubt very much it would remain so should they know you were here. Especially your son."

Anna watched her son, the king of dragons. The one that she had watched grow up since the moment she'd taken her last breath. Anna loved her boy. Loved, too, that he was so handsome and happy. But she'd made a promise to herself long ago that she'd not disrupt his life by going to see him. Even when he was small enough to have spoken to her.

"He is happy, is he not?" Austin, a ghost she'd known well in life, told her that Devon was happier than any of the others there. "My mother, she has done well with him. I've regretted only that he was responsible for killing his sire. However, he would never be the man he is should it have turned out differently."

"I know the same to be true of my own child. Bryce is what she is because of my death. I miss her. But like you, I can come to see them whenever I wish. It makes my heart feel a little fuller, knowing I can be nearby when I wish it. Are you sure you don't wish to meet him, Anna? It might well be the best thing for the two of you." Anna told him that she knew it would only make matters worse. "You have seen this then."

"I have." She'd seen a great deal while dying in her birthing bed. There weren't just scant pieces of his life that she'd seen, but it had played out in her mind as if she were there and a part of it. Anna knew that if she were to show herself to her only child, it would mean trouble for so many years. "He would be saddened by my leaving him. In that, his heart would be filled with sorrow, and he'd be hurtful to his mate. Kelly keeps him focused. If I were to show him that I see him and he could see me, all her work with him would be for naught. Things are better this way."

Anna also knew that should she show herself to Devon, it would set about a chain reaction that would only end in war, a war that she knew would expose him for what he really was, and the killing of dragons would begin anew. Her grandchildren would be hunted, the others as well. She wasn't entirely sure what brought the war to them, but when she saw his life without her in it, there was no strife, no wars, and more dragons to be born than even when there were more than humans.

Someone must have looked at the game they were watching, and the television was unmuted. Laughter slowed for a bit, and the cursing began. Even that she found wonderful. The colorful way each of them expressed their unhappiness with whatever was going on. Smiling at Austin, she leaned into his shoulder.

"When I was but a small child, I remember thinking of all the things I saw in my dreams. This, this box of news and movies was always playing a part in everyday life for everyone. I wish, at times, that it had never been invented. People use it to look at the outdoors more than they go out and enjoy it, I think." Austin said that was very true. "Then the small phones they use. I'm so happy to see that Devon has his guests drop them at the front door, so they're not distracted from whatever they're doing when visiting him. The others, they have done the same thing. Making sure that there are few distractions when they're all together."

"That is the reason, now that I think on it, that Bryce has put a spell around her home to make sure that no phones work when people are around. Laura, the love of my life, she will not use it to talk to anyone. She said if she has something to say to you, she will say it to your face. That way, there is no issue with things being read wrong. Laura is correct in that. Things said over text, they can be thought of in so many different ways." Austin asked her what she was going to do now. "Surely you're not going to stand here watching them when there are children about."

"I have visited each of the children that are a part of this family. It's wonderful that I can talk to them, and they listen." She moved out of the living room and ended up in the nursery. Kelly was there, rocking the small child that Anna had fallen deeply in love with. "You are my heart, little one."

Austin left her to rest. Since no one could see her, she didn't use as much energy as he had when visiting his family. Anna found her mother sitting in her room with her eyes closed. Going near her, she was startled when she began speaking. To her, it seemed.

"I miss you every single day, my darling." Anna was tempted to let her mother see her but decided she would wait. "I no longer go to the cemetery every day to talk to you but chat with you whenever I think of something to tell you about. How I wish you were here with us."

Her mother didn't look a day older than she had when Anna had been a child. Her hair was still dark and pulled back into a tight bun. Anna wondered what her mom would look like with it hanging down, the wind blowing through it. Laughing to herself, she knew that even if she were to have begged her to do that, her mom would have said it was undignified for a woman of her age to look so wanton. Sometimes her mother could be such a prude.

"You will be happy to know that I'm also helping the young women that have come to this family. They're strong ones, the mates to these boys. Such a mixture of magic that would have you happy with it. Pixies, faeries, witches, and humans. None of them are anything like you were. All of them, each and every one of them, would have knocked your husband down the stairs the first time he drew back to hit them." A tear rolled down her mother's cheek, and Anna wanted to wipe it away. "I believe you would have too, had that monster not chained you to the bed like an animal. He killed you. I know he did. He would have killed Devon, too, if the boy had not fought back. I know you're at peace with the way things turned out. But I so wish you could be here now to see him as a man. A king. A good person."

A faerie came in through the open window and sat upon Anna's mother's lap. She turned and looked at her. Anna put her fingers to her lips to tell the little one not to mention to her mother that she was there. When she nodded, the faerie turned back to her mom.

"Mistress? Mistress?" Mom opened her eyes and looked at the little person. "It is I, Lady Susanna. Lily."

Lily had been her faerie. All those years ago, it had been Lily that entertained her when she was alone. She even read books to her when Anna found herself too weak to even turn the pages. Watching as Lily waited on her mistress to wake fully, Anna wanted to have her read to her one more time.

"Lily. Thank you for waking me. I was having such a dream." Mom stood up, and Lily looked at Anna before going to her new mistress. "I had a dream that my Anna was just there, watching me as I did her when I was able. To think that she's been gone so long that I can still see her face as clearly as I had the day that she was born. What shall we do today?"

"The faeries have been putting the gardens in for the fallen dragons, my lady. They're all but finished with the ones that were found in the cave beyond. Also, I'm to tell you that your daughter's grave is now filled with faerie flowers too. That was a splendid idea that Lady Kelly had in marking her place in the world of dragons." Mom said she'd thought it a brilliant idea as well. "Lady Kelly said that was the place you first met her. At the grave of your daughter. We all think that the most romantic thing in the world. To have had the two of you meet in such a sad place."

"She was such a delight even then, you know. Why, she was even kind enough to say she'd come to tea with me sometime. But even then, I knew it wouldn't be so easy to get her to agree. She thought—still thinks even now sometimes—that she was unworthy of us. Imagine that. Kelly thinking she was less than us." Anna hadn't heard that story. She knew a lot about the story between her son and his mate. "Devon, he worships the ground she walks on. And Kelly.... Well, I don't think anyone loves their mate as well as she does my Devon."

When they left the bedroom to go to the gardens, Anna made her way to the place she'd come to vent her grievances. Her husband was there, the ground around him as dead as he was. None of the faeries would go to this place. No flowers grew around his grave. There was not even a headstone to mark his passing. Just a dark spot in the earth that grew darker with each passing year.

"Devon is doing well. He is happy too. Something that you never allowed any of us to be. You'll also be unhappy to hear that he is a good father and husband to his mate. Never once has he chained her to anything." Anna laughed a little. "Not that I think she'd allow him to do that. She is quite strong, you see. I believe with all my heart had you been alive when she came to the castle that she would have had you killed the very first day."

She often thought it funny that the dead would visit the dead. But Anna wanted to be assured that he heard every deed that her son had done. The way he took care of not only the good people in town but his friends as well.

"He's a good man, my son. Something that he thankfully decided to be on his own. You'll also feel that the earth loves him twice as much as they loathe you. You were a rotter, and I'm happy to see you here all alone in this place."

Anna looked around. There were no trees that bloomed in the summer here. No leaves that turned into beautiful shades of fall when the weather turned. Snow did not rest on this place, as the heat from the dead man below the earth didn't get flowers blooming in the spring. Nor did it have any fresh flowers put upon the grave when others would visit their loved one. No one, it seemed, cared enough to come and see to this man.

"Devon and his family will go on being happy. They will help millions of others with their time and money. There is nothing they won't do to make sure the people of the earth and the creatures that take care of it are well fed and warm when it's necessary." She thought of her grandchildren yet to come and those born already. "I believe that any of the children of these people would have run screaming from you. A child knows a monster better than most. You have nothing good to show for your time in Devon's life other than the sperm you used to create him. Thankfully, that is all you gave too."

Anna was getting tired. She had been out and about more today than she had in some time. It was time, she hated to admit that she went to rest. But she did have one more thing to say to the man she hated more than she did being dead all these years.

"This is the last time I will come here. The last time I will berate you for what you did to me and mine. I have come all these times to make it so you wallow in the goodness of Devon. The wonderful man that he became that you never were. My life and my death are no longer going to be attached to you in any way." She stood up. "Goodbye, you retched monster. I hope the hell you created for yourself is just as satisfying as I imagine it to be. May you never rest in peace."

Once she was back at her resting place, she felt stronger. Someone was thinking of her, and she had to smile. It was where the dead got their strength when someone thought of them. Glad to have spent the day as she had, Anna laid down to rest. Her family was happy. More happy than she had thought they'd ever be.

Before You Go...

HELP AN AUTHOR

write a review

THANK YOU!

Share your voice and help guide other readers to these wonderful books. Even if it's only a line or two, your reviews help readers discover the author's books so they can continue creating stories that you'll love. Log in to your favorite retailer and leave a review. Thank you.

AWARD WINNING, BESTSELLING AUTHOR

Kathi Barton, a winner of the Pinnacle Book Achievement award as well as a best-selling author on Amazon and All Romance books, lives in Nashport, Ohio, with her husband, Paul. When not creating new worlds and romance, Kathi and her husband enjoy camping and going to auctions. She can also be seen at county fairs with her husband, who is an artist and potter.

Her muse, a cross between Jimmy Stewart and Hugh Jackman, brings her stories to life for her readers in a way that has them coming back time and again for more. Her favorite genre is paranormal romance, with a great deal of spice. You can visit Kathi on line and drop her an email if you'd like. She loves hearing from her fans. aaronskiss@gmail.com.

Follow Kathi on her blog: http://kathisbartonauthor. blogspot.com/